CHRISTMAS BY THE LAKE

A COSY HOLIDAY NOVEL

MELISSA HILL

Originally published in 2014 as 'Christmas at the Heartbreak Cafe'
This edition © Little Blue Books, 2023

The right of Melissa Hill to be identified as the Author of the Work has been asserted by her in accordance with the Copyright, Designs and Patents Act 1988.

All rights reserved. No part of this publication may be reproduced, stored in a retrieval system, or transmitted, in any form or by any means without the prior written permission of the author. You must not circulate this book in any format.

All characters in this publication are fictitious and any resemblance to real persons, living or dead is purely coincidental.

CHAPTER 1

*E*lla Harris shuffled down Main Street at breakneck speed.

At sixty-two, she was still the same speed-walker as when much younger, and as she shot through the early crisp winter air, twinkling lights adorning the windows and roofs still-lit from the night before, flew past in a blur of red, white and green.

But Ella had no time to enjoy this sparkling festive display on the first day of December.

Instead, she had one thing on her mind: getting to her café on time. Nicknamed The Heartbreak Cafe by the locals for reasons that no one could no longer quite remember, it was the perfect lakeside gathering spot for world-weary residents and visiting tourists looking for a warm drink and an even warmer welcome.

The popular tourist town, twenty minutes drive from Dublin, was centred around a broad oxbow lake from which it took its name. The lake, surrounded by low-hanging beech and willow trees, wound its way around the centre, and a small humpback stone bridge joined all sides of the township together.

The cobbled streets and ornate lanterns on Main Street, as well as the beautiful one-hundred-year-old artisan cottages decorated with hanging floral baskets, had resulted in the village being designated heritage status by the Irish Tourist Board, and the chocolate-box look and feel was intentionally well preserved.

Ella's café was situated in a small two-storey building with an enviable position right at the edge of the lake and on the corner where the street began.

Early in their marriage, she and her husband took over the running of the café from her father-in-law, and she spent nearly every waking moment since then ensuring that his legacy—and that of her dearly departed husband Gregory—lived on through good food, hot coffee, and warm conversation.

The interior hadn't changed much over the years — it was still a warm cosy room with parquet oak flooring, shelves full of dried flowers and old country-style knick-knacks, along with haphazard seating and mismatched tables, one of which was an antique Singer sewing table.

In front of the kitchen and serving area was a long granite countertop, where various solo customers typically nursed their coffees and pastries atop a row of stools. Alongside this was a glass display case filled with a selection of freshly baked goods; muffins, doughnuts, carrot cake, brownies and cream puffs for the sweet-toothed, and pies, sausage rolls and Italian breads for the more savoury-orientated.

From early morning the place was flooded with families, friends and neighbours, all there to grab a bite to eat—and to gossip. Ella thrived on the commotion and excitement, and the community had embraced her; she had become a figurehead in the town and a confidant to anyone who came in looking for a bit of conversation with their coffee.

But her job was never easy. The early morning start meant that Ella was up at 5 am to make the mile-long trek from her home on the other side of town, across the humpback stone bridge over the lake to the café's kitchen.

This morning, she was running atypically late. Late—it was such an unfamiliar word. She hadn't slept late in nearly twenty years. She was gripped with an unsettling feeling of panic as she checked her watch.

6:15. *Damn,* she thought to herself.

This was going to be tight. She could certainly get the coffee started, and set her chef Colm's baked breakfast favourites out on display, but would she have time to get the tables set and fried breakfasts prepped before her first customer arrived? Breakfast choices at the café typically ranged from yoghurt, muesli and bagels, to the Full Irish heart attack of fried sausages, mushrooms, eggs bacon and hash browns, complete with locally produced black pudding.

Ella turned her quick walk into a half-jog. It

was tight because many of her early-morning regulars were residents commuting to work in Dublin so she'd better pick up the pace.

She was speeding around the corner by the edge of the walkway to the lake when she felt her right shoe slip from underneath her. She grabbed for the silver tinsel hanging from the nearby lamppost when her left foot turned the other way and her back moved in reverse in an almost pained slow motion. Then swirled in an almost elegant three-quarter turn and was suddenly staring skyward, her back on the ground.

Ouch.

She inched herself off the pavement and quickly looked around her, stunned and a little embarrassed.

Thank goodness, she thought, seeing no other early morning walkers around. Using her hands for support and leverage, she pushed herself upright and onto her feet. But as soon as she leaned her body weight on the right side, she let out a yelp. Her ankle had failed her.

She briefly cursed her love of old-fashioned Mary Jane heels and her neglectful landlord who always 'forgot' to salt the path in frosty weather.

Pride battered somewhat more than her ankle, Ella hopped on one foot the rest of the way to the café.

CHAPTER 2

As she opened the side entrance, she wondered what she should do now. Colm wasn't due in until later, so she had no other choice but to close for the morning—maybe even longer? She certainly couldn't get through the busy breakfast rush and beyond all by herself.

Still, Ella prided herself on being independent and never asking for help. Now she had to though, and the thought of it was both disheartening and frightening.

As she sat in the café's darkened kitchen with her ankle elevated on a nearby chair, she teared up at the thought of having to call a taxi to bring herself to the hospital.

Just as she began to fall into a pit of despair, she heard a knock at the door out front.

"We're still closed, sorry!" she called back at the stranger. The knocking suddenly stopped and then she heard heavy footsteps moving away. She let out a sigh of relief as she dropped her bad leg to the ground and used her arms and better leg to anchor her to stand again. Then slowly made her way to where she'd left her handbag, and as she rummaged through it for her phone, the knocking started up again. This time at the lakeside door to the side of the kitchen, and the knock was forceful and urgent.

"Ella! Are you in there? Are you all right?"

The voice was gruff, yet had a tinge of obvious concern, and she instantly recognised who was calling out. That distinct, gravelly voice belonged to her most loyal customer, Joseph Evans.

The owner of Lakeview Riding School and Stables, Joseph had been visiting the café every Monday since he was the new person in town almost thirty years before, about the same time as Ella and Gregory took over the café.

Even though he lived a little way outside

the village, he still stopped in faithfully every morning for a blueberry scone and a cup of coffee.

"Joseph? Is that you? Give me a second."

Ella dropped the handbag on the table, quickly smoothed a hand over her freshly braided hair and realigned her dress. With all her might, she managed to use the tables and counter space to limp towards the side entrance.

As she opened the door, she caught a familiar earthy smell from the man towering over her—fresh pine trees and grass. His grey hair almost sparkled as gently falling snow touched the strands. Joseph had yet to lose the rugged good looks that had made him quite the catch in Lakeview for many years. Yet he'd never married.

"You sounded flustered," he said gently as she opened the door wider. "You're never flustered."

"Oh," she said, blushing slightly, "it's—um—"

"What happened?" he asked. "Baking accident? Tell me it wasn't the scones…" The lighthearted humour in his voice made Ella forget to wonder what he was doing there.

She shook her head bashfully. "It's nothing. I just slid on the ice out front. You would think that Paul would have salted the paths, but you know how cheap he is," she added referring to her landlord, a wealthy banker who owned the buildings housing most of the local businesses on Main Street.

"Ella," Joseph insisted, catching her grimace, "it's obviously *not* nothing. You're hurt. Why didn't you call an ambulance?"

"An ambulance?" she asked, attempting to smile. "I don't need an ambulance. I was just going to call a taxi to come pick me up and bring me to Jim Kelly to see if he'd put a bandage on it. It's *not* that big a deal. I mean, I can still walk…"

"Not a big deal?" he said sardonically, looking down at her leg. "You can't even put any weight on it. I'm sure Dr Kelly will agree and send you straight to A & E."

"But I can," she insisted.

"Prove it," he challenged her.

Ella slowly lowered her foot, steadied her leg and leaned to the side. The pain instantly shot through her body and she let out a loud squeal and stumbled forward. Joseph grabbed her arm as she nearly tumbled into his chest. Obviously, her pride had once again got the best of her.

"Okay, yeah," he said, holding her up and shaking his head. "I'm taking you to the hospital myself. You can pay me back in scones and coffee when you're back on your feet."

Ella reluctantly nodded. Joseph helped her back onto the chair and quickly ran out the side door to retrieve his Land Rover. As she waited, she made a list of all the things she would need to do to get the café opened this afternoon.

Maybe she could just serve drinks instead of food today? That would keep her off her feet mostly. Though she really should serve food, considering that Monday was always her most profitable day.

Ella knew that she had to alert her staff one way or another, so she quickly jotted down a note to Colm and a small waiting crew that explained why she wasn't in this morning. She trusted her chef to handle all in her absence. Colm had worked for her since he was an awkward teenage boy nearly fifteen years ago.

The lights of a vehicle suddenly flooded through the back window and Joseph hurried inside.

"OK," he said, a braced look on his face, "I know it's not the best plan but I need to get you into the jeep, so I'm going to have to pick you up."

"No," she said, blushing again. "I'm like a sack of spuds."

"You have a better idea?"

"Crane?" she joked.

Joseph smiled and shook his head. "I'm not taking no for an answer."

Without another word, he reached for Ella's arms and gently stood her up and out of the chair. Then with one fluid and steady motion, he picked her up and grabbed her handbag as he carried her over the side-door threshold and into his humming vehicle.

CHAPTER 3

The drive to the hospital was breathtaking. Rarely did Ella take a moment to take in the picturesque beauty of her hometown. But as the snow fell sparingly on the windshield and the old-fashioned street lamps glittered in the darkness, she felt a fondness for Lakeview that she hadn't experienced in years.

Christmas by the lake had always been a special time growing up here. Ice skating on the frozen water, hot chocolate and the town's fun and festive parades.

Ella's then-future father-in-law's café would transform into a lakeside gathering place for the then-much smaller community, which all came together to celebrate the festive season. There were carriage rides by the lake shore, a jolly Santa Claus, plenty of mince pies, homemade mulled wine and general joviality through the streets.

At the end of an evening, local musicians would play a combination of traditional Irish and Christmas music—the kind that made you fall in love with the season all over again, and as she remembered one particular night dancing cheek to cheek with Gregory, her soon-to-be husband, Ella raised a wistful smile.

"Your ankle must not be hurting as much now," Joseph murmured.

"Hmmm?" She broke out of her nostalgic musings to acknowledge him.

"You're smiling." He winked as he took his eyes off the road momentarily.

"Ah, I was just remembering those old Christmas parties we used to have by the lake and how special they were. Were you around for those?"

"I was for the last few before it all stopped. They were great. Always loved the mulled wine—especially the stronger version that came out after the kids left." He laughed heartily at the memory. "Why don't you do that kind of thing anymore? I'm sure the community would love it."

"Gregory used to drive it mostly. That all stopped after he died." Her voice dropped to a whisper. She hadn't said her husband's name out loud in quite a while.

"Oh, I'm sorr—"

"Don't be. Once he passed away, his father and I didn't have it in us to take on all the organising of it. Those were the days though." Ella looked off into the distance.

"But why not now?" Joseph asked, breaking a short silence.

"What do you mean?"

"Why not think about another lakeside Christmas celebration now?" He looked at her earnestly, excitement glimmering in his dark brown eyes. "By my reckoning, the café is coming up to thirty years in business with you at the helm. Good enough reason to celebrate too, no?"

"Ah, I'm way too old for that kind of thing. I would need so much help, and I can't—"

"Can't imagine asking for help?" He rolled his eyes. "When are you going to understand that this town adores you, Ella? They love the café and you. I'm pretty sure that everybody in the community, including myself, would only be too delighted to get involved. Just think about it maybe?"

Ella sank back into the jeep's heated seats. She had to admit the idea of throwing an old-style celebration was very tempting, especially given the year that was in it.

Joseph was right; she had indeed been in business in Lakeview for thirty years and a Christmas party would be a lovely way to show gratitude to the community for their support over that time.

But if she was going to do this and do it right, she would have to ask for help. She could do that, maybe? Just like Joseph said, there wasn't a soul in Lakeview that Ella couldn't turn to.

It was all about finding the right people.

As the two pulled up to the hospital's Emergency Room doors, Joseph idled the jeep in the entryway. He swung around to Ella's passenger side door and offered his arm. As he hoisted her gently out of the seat, she sighed.

"You know what, Joseph, I'm going to do it.

I am going to organise a thank you Christmas party for my customers this year. You're right, it would be amazing. But I'm going to need your help with one particular task all the same."

"What's that?" he asked as he carried her like a child into the ER waiting room.

"Oh, you'll see soon enough. First, I need to figure out the rest of it."

Despite the soreness, Ella smiled brightly as the thought of all that she needed to do and prepare danced in her head.

Like her beloved Gregory used to say, she always did love a challenge.

CHAPTER 4

*R*uth Seymour sped towards Lakeview like a madwoman. Tree limbs flew past her car window in a fury of pine green and icy white. Music blared from her SUV's speakers as she loudly sang along, belting out every high note she could reach.

Driving was Ruth's therapy. Ever since she gave up her LA movie career and returned home almost two years ago, she needed to be in the driver's seat more and more.

Speeding along the tree-lined roads and gravel pathways of the back routes around her hometown was a stark contrast from her old stomping ground of Los Angeles.

She enjoyed the freedom and relative

anonymity that came with small-town life though. It was all Ruth could do to keep from bursting with happiness as she steered pin-tight corners, and now she rolled her windows down to feel the crisp and clean wintry air on her face.

Luckily for her, the lack of a major police presence and the complete absence of photographers made it easy for her to indulge in her vice without much care or worry.

One time she'd been pulled over on the road to Dublin for speeding but the cop let her go once he recognised her as the star of popular US TV show, *Glamazons*. But that was a couple of years ago and these days Ruth was no longer quite as famous.

Or indeed glamorous.

She slowed the car as the outskirts of the town loomed and the houses grew closer together, and soon she neared the old secondary school.

Even just driving past, she was flooded with memories of her former school days. She remembered her very first dramatic solo, a musical piece in Latin. Her singing had received a standing ovation and requests that she perform at local weddings and funerals for years to come.

And then there was her first play. As a mere second-year, she had landed the lead role in *Evita*. It was challenging at first as she struggled to learn all of the songs and cues, but she would never forget the crowd rising to their feet in applause as she hit the final big note in *Don't Cry for Me Argentina*.

Then, of course, she could never forget the day she met Charlie Mellon.

How he'd idly sauntered past her in the school hallway. She was surrounded by her gaggle of friends—a group that never left her side. Two years older and devastatingly handsome with a leather jacket and a confident smile, Ruth was immediately smitten and determined to make him hers.

A few days later, she found him standing outside a classroom waiting for the bell to ring. Taking a deep breath, she'd casually strolled up to him, flashed her most radiant smile and asked if he could help her with her Maths homework.

"It would be *such* a favour," she chirped. "I can't seem to get through this by myself."

He just stared at her for several seconds, studying her face with a quizzical look. Then offered his hand to her—a formality so rare that it reminded her of those old black-and-white romance movies. Ruth practically swooned. As they made plans for their study sessions, he never once took his eyes off of her. Unlike the rest of the boys who wouldn't even dare look her in the eye, his unassuming confidence made her feel shy again. Her face reddened, her palms sweated and her heart raced.

They spent the next few months studying together without any romantic overtures. Sometimes Ruth would lean into him as she turned the page, but he never returned the affection. Only once did he touch her hand as they both grabbed for a pencil at the same time.

Ruth was about to give up on Charlie ever making a move until their final week before the Christmas break. It was a few short days away from the holidays. As she went to meet him in the secluded study area of the town's library, she braced herself for another session with Serious Charlie. But he wasn't at their usual table. Instead, a handwritten note was on the chair:

Ruth,

I THOUGHT WE COULD HAVE A CHANGE OF PACE FOR TODAY. I'M SICK OF THE LIBRARY. MEET ME AT ELLA'S WHEN YOU GET THIS. FOOD'S ON ME.

— CHARLIE.

She'd grabbed her schoolbag and ran through the town square onto Main Street towards the café, The Heartbreak Cafe some of the older girls called it. Hopefully nothing like heartbreak awaited Ruth there today.

Through the window, she could see Charlie sitting at the granite counter, chatting casually with the owner. She strolled in confidently and took a seat next to him, waving a friendly hello to Ella, who smiled knowingly and made herself scarce.

"Well, this is a lovely change from the library," Ruth smiled. 'What made you think of this?"

"I just felt like something sweet. Ella makes the best muffins in the universe. Have you tried them?"

"No, believe it or not, I've actually never

been in here before. It's really cool though." She studied the old-world decor. It wasn't exactly her style, but it had real charm, complete with cosy details. The wall's pink and green accents reminded her of the movie sets for technicolour musicals. The mix-matched china teacups were even out of date in a way that was comforting. It was almost like she had stepped into her grandmother's front room.

"I'll order you something. How about tea, a muffin, and a piece of Twix cake? My mate, Colm works here at weekends and he has some new recipe he's been bugging us all about. Ella finally let him stock it, so it must be good."

Ruth nodded in agreement and Charlie casually rattled off the order. Without much time to change the subject, the café owner was back again with two muffins from the back. As she placed the food down in front of them, she winked at Ruth as if she knew exactly what was going on, and Ruth duly blushed for the second time in her life.

In the middle of sips and bites, Charlie broke the silence, "So, I don't think you need to cram anymore. You're going to do fine on the Maths test."

"Easy for you to say. You know it all. I've never met someone as brilliant. You should do something like programme a space launch. The world needs more of you."

"Nothing that high-falutin," he chuckled. "I want to be a mechanic actually. I love figuring out how things work."

"A mechanic? That's amazing." Ruth flirtatiously sipped her coffee, all the while keeping her eyes locked on his, though she privately thought that he was aiming a little low. A boring old mechanic when he could easily be some kind of high-ranking engineer in Dublin, or London even?

When she suggested as much, he smiled.

"Well, as much as the money might be nice, I'll probably just stay here in Lakeview. Nothing too glamorous like you have in mind for yourself."

"Like I have in mind?"

"Yeah, I'm imagining you in New York—a big Broadway star or something. Give it ten years and your name will be everywhere."

Ruth smiled at this. It wasn't hard for anyone to guess that she had her eyes on something bigger and brighter than Lakeview, yet no one had ever said it so confidently to her.

"Yes. I want to be a star. Doing what, I'm not sure. But I plan on having my name in lights somehow. Maybe an Oscar or a Grammy, even." She grinned from ear to ear.

"Speaking of which, I have a gift for you," Charlie said. Something for Christmas. Open it."

He handed her a flat gift box wrapped in red tissue and a white bow. Her name was neatly printed on a tag.

Ruth's heart skipped a beat as she gently tore the paper. She didn't want to seem too eager. As she opened the box, she began to tear up. Inside was a framed piece of sheet music. It was the score to *Don't Cry for Me Argentina*.

"Last year, I saw you in the play. Your voice was beautiful. I had never heard anything like that in my entire life." He stared at her with his grey piercing eyes waiting for a response, but Ruth was so overwhelmed, all she could do was gently rub her hands on the gold, metal frame. Tears fell onto the glass.

Before she knew it, she stood up, reached for Charlie Mellon's face and kissed him. It was soft and gentle, but her mouth lingered on his until he wrapped his arm around her waist and his other around the back of her head. The café's stereo played the old Dean Martin Christmas classic, *I've Got My Love to Keep Me Warm*.

It was Charlie and Ruth's first kiss, but it certainly wouldn't be their last. They were together for the remainder of their time in secondary school and beyond. Then afterwards he went to work in his family's car dealership, and before long Ruth was bound for Dublin for an audition for a soap opera produced by an Irish TV station. With a heavy heart, they said their goodbyes and promised in earnest to keep in touch.

Twelve years later, and Ruth could still feel the pain of those final moments together. First love was always the hardest to let go of, but luckily for Ruth, she got a second chance. While Charlie remained in Lakeview, eventually growing the dealership and taking over, Ruth had moved up from the soap opera world and moved to LA full-time.

After a few bit parts in movies, she became a regular star in *Glamazons*. But after a brief ill-advised affair with her co-star Troy, she found out she was pregnant and returned home to figure out what to do next.

Despite her problems, she and Charlie managed to reunite, and when little Scarlett was born a few months later, Charlie was by Ruth's side.

Troy had refused to visit or even acknowledge the birth of his daughter, whereas Charlie jumped in and assisted Ruth with the first few weeks of feedings, nappy changes, and bath times. At this point, she had quit LA and moved back to Lakeview.

Life it seemed had other, more important plans for her.

Scarlett had just turned twelve months when Charlie proposed. She was already walking, and one night she occasionally stopped, looked at Charlie and stumbled into his arms for a hug or a quick snuggle before she was back at it again. After several moments of this, Charlie took her aside and whispered something in her ear. The baby toddled into the kitchen where Ruth was reading over a script and tugged at her hand.

"What is it, sweetie?" Ruth asked, following

her daughter into the living room. Charlie had moved off of the couch and onto one knee. In his hands were two rings. One was made from candy and the other was a diamond that shone so bright it glimmered from several feet away.

"Ruth and Scarlett—I cannot imagine my life without the two of you. I need you both with me here. Will you, the two of you - marry me?"

Little Scarlett held her mother's hand, shyly looking up at her for permission to go and take the sweet.

"Oh my goodness, YES!" Ruth squealed as she ran into Charlie's arms while Scarlett followed right behind her, deftly grabbing for the candy as she moved into their embrace.

CHAPTER 5

*N*ow, as Ruth pulled into the lakeside parking area near the cafe, she took a moment to think about how different her life was these days. No longer was she living in a swanky Hollywood Hills townhouse or hobnobbing with celebrities. She'd rarely signed a single autograph since moving in with Charlie to his house just outside town. Still, she was happy—she truly was.

Except for one little problem.

Think of the devil ... Ruth walked into the café and spotted *her*. Sitting at the counter chatting with Ella was an older woman dressed in black from head to toe. Her hair was piled into a neat, old-fashioned bun at the top of her head and she sipped her tea with her pinky finger out as if she were way more important than she was.

Ruth gritted her teeth. She was *not* going to let Charlie's mother ruin her much-needed morning latte. She walked in confidently, strolled to a table on the other side of the room and faced away from her nemesis. Her face flushed as she could feel Ita staring daggers at her back.

Ella today using a cane, hobbled to her table, "Ruth, love. What can I get you?"

"Oh, Ella, I heard about your ankle. You poor thing! Why aren't you sitting in the back resting and letting Colm take over?"

"Too much to do! And it's only a sprain. I'll be back at it in a week or two. Did you hear about my bringing back the old Christmas party? You, Charlie, and Scarlett will come, yes?"

"A party? We certainly will be there, with bells on. Is there anything I can do to help?"

"Actually now that you say it, I am in need of a singer. A party wouldn't be any good without a singsong. And everyone in Lakeview just loves to hear you sing. You'd just need to do some Christmas favourites and a few ballads."

"Ha, not a chance," Ita Mellon piped up from her seat at the counter. "It wouldn't be good enough for Madam Hollywood unless you plan on inviting the paparazzi and maybe Elvis. Isn't that right, dear?"

Ruth shuttered in embarrassment and anger. She was used to her mother-in-law's snide comments about her former life, but it stung nonetheless. She knew that Ita was furious that Charlie chose to marry her and adopt Scarlett instead of finding his own (baggage-free) wife here in town. Never mind that Charlie was Scarlett's father through and through.

But to Ita, Ruth was just some tramp who'd trapped her beloved son into raising a child that was not his.

"Ella, I would be honoured," she smiled graciously. "When is the event happening?"

"Evening of December 22, just in time for Christmas. We'll have a big celebration; food, mulled wine, Santa and hopefully bring back carriage rides around the lake for the kids too if we can arrange it, so be sure to bring little Scarlett along."

"We'll be there, I promise. But in the meantime," she smiled apologetically. "I'm starving and in a bit of a rush. I have to pick up Scarlett from the creche in a half hour. Can I get a latte and a pain au chocolat to take away?"

"Certainly, pet."

Ella toddled off, leaving Ita and Ruth to both stew in their collective corners of the café.

Maybe Ruth agreeing to take part in something like this party might help Ita see that she loved Charlie and had every intention of staying in Lakeview. And in turn might cause Ita to treat Scarlett as her granddaughter instead of a complete stranger. Ruth knew it really hurt Charlie that his mother still wouldn't acknowledge them as family, even after all this time.

She sighed. Though at this point, she wasn't sure if anything could repair their relationship.

Taking out her Prada purse to pay for the food, Ruth's eyes rested on the script nestled in there that had arrived from her agent only that morning.

The fact that she was of late considering a return to work in Tinseltown, certainly wouldn't improve matters.

CHAPTER 6

*H*eidi Clancy was running late. After spending a very pleasant morning in Dublin getting her hair and nails done, she was stuck behind the slow-moving trucks of the old timber yard just outside the town.

Currently, her car, a brand new black BMW, was idling behind a large red semi carrying at least a dozen unruly pine trunks. It took everything in Heidi's power not to honk her horn, but she resisted out of fear of breaking her nails.

Behind her outward impatience was a smidgen of satisfaction though. While being late was typically a social sin, being late to an occasion like the Lakeview Mum's Club did have its benefits.

Heidi knew that her late entrance to Cynthia Roland's house in which they were holding today's gathering, would be fawned over, with the crowd of women asking her about traffic and her morning.

Everyone would rise to make a fuss of her gorgeous daughter Amelia, grab her box of 'homemade' cupcakes and remark at her brand new DVF coat. Attention would be all hers and Heidi certainly knew how to milk it.

But most importantly, her *absence* would have everyone talking. The girls couldn't resist an opportunity to gossip about the village's richest woman.

Well, maybe the second richest. Ever since that soap star moved back home, it was all that the town's gossip crowd could chat about. If they weren't whispering about Ruth Seymour's scandalous affair with her co-star, they were discussing how much her Hollywood Hills townhouse must have sold for.

Heidi did not mind the competition one bit; it gave her an excuse to step up her game. She had already laid out plans to redecorate the living room of their palatial home on the Dublin Road and add on separate living quarters for their live-in nanny.

Her bank manager husband Paul certainly couldn't resist when she asked to borrow his credit card for a day at the salon because hers was already maxed out. Whatever Heidi wanted, Heidi got and she was never afraid to ask for more.

Finally past the literal logjam of timber trucks, Heidi put the pedal to the floor. She still had to pop by the house to collect little Amelia and the nanny, and she also had to make it to Ella's Cafe to pick up some of Colm's special cupcakes. She had to hurry if she wanted to make a fashionably late entrance and avoid being outright rude though.

Luckily for her, Miriam and Amelia were already waiting for her on the porch. The nanny had a pained look on her face that Heidi shrugged off with a couple of insincere apologies and promised to let her know when she would be late in the future.

Amelia, on the other hand, was as pleasant as ever. At only two years old, her daughter had a glow that never failed to put a smile on

Heidi's face. As expected, she was a natural at motherhood and found it hard to believe that after all the related fuss of her sister Cara's wedding - whereupon a heavily pregnant Heidi had to travel to St Lucia to watch her sister walk down the aisle - that she'd still managed to retain a level head and good spirits for the remainder of her pregnancy.

Though in truth, she and her sister had a much better relationship these days, and while Heidi and her sister-in-law Kim still like to engage in an occasional war of words, they too had managed a truce of sorts, made easier by the fact Amelia and Kim's son Jago, were the same age.

With the nanny in the back of the car entertaining Amelia, Heidi was soon back on the road. As she parked directly onto double yellow lines directly outside Ella's café (her husband owned the building so she was within her rights), her phone began to ring.

Checking the caller ID, she sighed. Her sister-in-law from the other side of the family, Gemma, Paul's youngest sibling. And a pure Mummy Martyr.

She spent her time at the club complaining

about how hard it was to raise her twins and spent hours counting pennies and avoiding a much-needed facial. It was so tiring—so much so that she routinely ignored Gemma's calls. Today would not be an exception.

Heidi raced inside the café to meet Ella at the counter. Her Lucy Choi heels clinked loudly on the wooden floor enough that the noise caught the attention of the rest of the customers. "Hello Ella, do you have my order ready? I'm running forty minutes late already."

"Of course I do. We never forget your orders." Ella answered, a bit wounded.

"Thank you soooo much!" Heidi flashed her ultra-bright white smile at the older woman and quickly handed her Paul's platinum credit card.

"Now that I have you, when you get a chance - with all the frost we're getting lately - can you please ask Paul to salt the paths out front?" Ella's tone was gently scolding, but Heidi was too busy checking her reflection in the display glass casing. "I twisted my ankle the other day and am on crutches for the next month. I understand he's busy but he really should get someone to do that if he can't come to do it himself."

"Oh, yeah. I will as soon as I see him," the younger girl replied, absent-mindedly.

'Um...sorry Heidi, but the card has been declined,' Ella said then looking apologetic and Heidi immediately jumped to attention.

"What? But that's impossible! I just used it this morning and — " She rummaged in her wallet for some cash.

"Not to worry, sure you can sort me out some other time...." Waving the incident away, Ella smiled and handed her back the card.

"Are you sure? It's just I don't usually carry cash and — "

Flustered, Heidi felt her cheeks redden. This could *not* be happening. She hadn't gone too crazy in the city this morning had she? Yes, she'd been stocking up on Christmas presents (to say nothing of her own wardrobe) but it was a platinum card for goodness sake, the limit must be sky high. If there even was a limit ... Heidi couldn't understand it.

"Thank you. I'll pop back later when I've been to a cashpoint. *Au revoir!*" she called as she flipped her hair and strutted towards the door with the cupcake box in her free arm.

"OK, let's roll guys - mummy time!" Heidi proclaimed as she belted herself in, checked her lipstick and backed out of the space, the incident with the credit card already forgotten.

CHAPTER 7

Cynthia Roland's house was next door to Heidi's sister-in-law's. Nestled in a modest estate, the house looked exactly like all the other boring others in the development.

Apart from the number of cars in the driveway and the sign on the front lawn, Heidi wouldn't have even begun to guess which house she was supposed to be headed towards.

As she parked the car, she noticed the women inside subtly staring at her from the window. *This* was exactly the entrance she wanted. She confidently strolled in, carrying the cupcakes with Miriam and Amelia about ten feet behind.

"Cynthia, darling. You look fabulous as

always!" Heidi crowed at the sight of the pale, meek woman answering the door.

"Not as good as you, I'm afraid." Her friend's insincere smile did nothing to faze Heidi as she was greeted by a gaggle of women, all ready and eager to applaud her presence.

"Let me take that from you!"

"Oh! Look at your jacket! Is it new?"

"Who did your hair? It looks *perfect*."

"You shouldn't have gone to the trouble of baking all these, Heidi! It's too kind of you."

"How is Paul? I hear you bought *another* building in town recently."

"Your nails are the most *gorgeous* shade. I wish I was bold enough to wear that colour."

As the compliments rolled in, Heidi effortlessly swivelled back and forth to give each woman her answer and a polite peck on the cheek.

All except Gemma. While the rest of the Mum's Club had greeted her at the door, her sister-in-law had remained seated in a chair by the fireplace. She was staring daggers at Heidi, but her look significantly softened as she spotted Miriam and Amelia walking through the door.

"Miriam, let me take Amelia from you. I never get enough time with her when I visit. And you must be exhausted taking care of her all by yourself day in and day out." Gemma proclaimed loudly so that each of the other mums would hear her.

The women moved from Heidi and then began to swoon over Amelia. While Gemma's barb should have ruffled Heidi, it only boosted her self-importance that much more.

After the greetings and compliments were sufficiently dispensed, Heidi led the gang back into the living area. Taking her place at the front of the room, she watched as Amelia gingerly toddled towards the other children to play with the plethora of toys assembled.

"So, what was your day like Heidi?" asked a woman she vaguely recognised but couldn't be bothered to remember her name.

"Oh… the usual. I went to Dublin to get my nails done at the BT Nail Bar, and while there dropped an absolute *fortune* on the second floor. Then I went to have my hair done at Hair Box before picking up Paul's suits from the dry cleaner, and I just about managed to get in a light workout before heading out earlier. It's been such a busy day already!"

"If only I could manage to get to the gym," sighed another woman Heidi avoided.

"It's all about priorities, really. You can do it if you set your mind to it." She smiled at her own encouragement.

"You mean, you could set your mind to it if you had plenty of money and a live-in nanny, and a cleaner?" A couple of the women giggled as Gemma snarked. "You have to admit that you have it lucky with Paul's money paying for everything. You don't have to lift a finger."

"I suppose, but he does work hard and we have the same worries as everyone else. I just don't talk about them non-stop." Heidi felt a bit defensive at the insinuation that her life was easy.

"Not all of us marry for money. Some of us do so for love." Gemma's comments came across as a slap in the face. While Heidi had known that her sister-in-law harboured resentment towards her, she had never heard her express it so openly or in such a public space before.

She could do nothing but look down at her

shoes. Which of course was no great hardship either.

"Did you girls hear about Ella's big Christmas party? I remember those special days of Christmas when I was a little girl," Cynthia interjected, breaking the awkward silence that had fallen after Heidi and Gemma's sparring.

"Really? A party? Here in Lakeview?" asked one of the other mothers whose baby was currently drooling contentedly in her arms.

Heidi was intrigued. Any social occasion piqued her interest, especially if it gave her a chance to do a little good old-fashioned showing off.

"Yes. The old Christmas parties used to be great fun. Free food, drinks, music, and lots going on for the kids. The whole town would turn out." Cynthia practically beamed at the memory.

"Where on earth is Ella hosting this shindig? Maybe in the old days it was fine, but she certainly couldn't fit the entire town in that tiny café now."

Heidi thought Gemma had an excellent point and it got her thinking.

"I know," she interjected, deciding. "Our house. It's the only one big enough. We already have our own marquee and I'm working with a party coordinator now about where to place everything, but I am thinking red and green linen with poinsettia centrepieces accented with mistletoe, of course…"

The last bit was a bald-faced lie, but she was sure Ella Harris would only jump at the chance to save herself the bother of holding a messy gathering at the café following any lakeside festive activities if that was the plan.

Gemma kept her eyes squarely on Heidi as she continued to ramble off her imagined plans for the Christmas party. She suspected instantly that Heidi was lying, but she held her tongue.

As the women chatted excitedly about the upcoming celebrations, Heidi excused herself to the bathroom. Sneaking upstairs, she quietly dialled Ella's number.

"This is Ella speaking." The soft voice momentarily soothed Heidi. "Hello?"

"Ella, Heidi here. I just heard that you were bringing back the Christmas by the lake party night to celebrate your thirtieth year in business. Is that true?" She couldn't come across as too eager.

"Oh, hello, Heidi," Ella said in a significantly lower tone, her voice suddenly losing its friendly chirp. "That's right, I am indeed throwing a little shindig on December 22nd. You, Paul, and Amelia are certainly invited."

"That's great! Do you have a location in mind for the party itself?"

"Well naturally I was thinking the café and -"

Heidi cut her off, ready to pounce. "No, no, no. The café is way too small. I insist that your party be at our home. As your landlord, Paul would be only too delighted to allow you to do so for free. We will arrange the marquee, the tables, the heating, everything! Guests can use our bathrooms and your staff can set up in our kitchen. It will be more than enough room for the whole town."

The silence that followed was almost deafening. If Ella said no, she wouldn't know what to do. "And naturally we'll arrange to have someone in for the clean-up afterwards. Honestly, do you really want your café to be subjected to such upheaval, especially so close to Christmas?"

"I suppose you have a point and there will be a lot more people …" Ella trailed off, Heidi's words obviously hitting home. "Are you sure Paul is on board with this?"

"Yes, we insist!" Heidi reiterated as loudly as she could without potentially drawing attention to herself.

"All right then. How about you pop back in soon, and we'll discuss it."

"It's a plan. Chat with you soon, Ella."

Heidi hung up, tucked her phone back into her pocket and strolled confidently back into the living room. Her smile was as bold as ever as she practically burst in anticipation.

Not only would she be hosting the most talked-about Lakeview party in years, but she would be doing it in her own gorgeous house in front of the whole community.

Heidi lived for opportunities like these.

CHAPTER 8

Ella had spent much of the following week listening to Heidi's plans for what she proclaimed to be the "The Lakeview social outing of the century!"

Reluctant at first to relinquish the reins to someone as disconnected from the essence of the community as Heidi (despite being born and bred here and the daughter of one of Ella's closest friends) she had nevertheless been impressed with just how devoted the young woman seemed to be. Truth be told Ella was actually a little relieved to have someone deal with the finer event details other than food and music.

During the first meeting, Betty Clancy's

youngest rambled on about tableware choices (pintuck, red silk, extra long table runners, etc.) while pouring through sample books from party planning companies. The joy she seemed to take from hosting was infectious as Ella grew more and more excited for the big day to arrive.

They ended the meeting agreeing on invitation layouts and the best way to distribute them.

Debbie from Amazing Days Design, proprietor of the local stationery designer business, would be tasked with creating a specially commissioned invite incorporating Christmas by the lake and the café's thirty-year anniversary celebrations.

Heidi would also ask her to create matching fliers for Ella to hang in the café and distribute around to make sure everyone in the village knew about the party. It seemed as if no stone would be left unturned when it came to this 'collaboration'.

But the second meeting felt vastly different by comparison. Heidi was distracted and dare Ella say it, a bit dishevelled, even.

Her nail polish was chipped, her hair

appeared uncoiffed, and she looked as though she hadn't been sleeping very well. Did this maybe have something to do with the declined credit card from before? she wondered.

Despite herself, Ella felt a little sorry for Heidi. It had to be hard to keep up appearances all the time. While she herself couldn't care less about things like jewellery, Mummy clubs, or professional garden maintenance, she did understand that Heidi's self-created reputation was constantly at stake when she stepped out in public.

Nonetheless, Heidi ploughed through the meeting with few breaks for chit-chat. She made a couple of notes about changes she had made and occasionally snuck in a remark about the price of items like lighting or silk napkins.

Ella could easily pick up that Heidi seemed to be avoiding a much bigger topic, but she wouldn't be the one to bring it up.

Instead, Ella had spent the meeting mentally planning out the menu. There would be café favourites from down through the years, mince pies and cupcakes decorated as Christmas presents, cookies in the shape of toys and snowmen, traditional Irish Christmas fruitcake and pudding, and a mulled wine recipe that would make her father-in-law proud.

Beforehand down by the lake, they would bring out mini burners so that hungry children and adults alike could roast marshmallows to dip in chocolate.

While Heidi ended the second meeting with a long face, Ella felt practically euphoric. The thought of all the cooking ahead of her didn't break her spirit. Instead, it gave her life and purpose that she had not felt in years. She couldn't help but rush into the kitchen to chat with Colm about her plans.

Before she could make it to the back of the café, one of her staff members handed her some letters that had come in the post earlier that morning. Mainly junk.

Ella quickly sorted through it with a fine eye for bills and important notes. Until a mailing from the estate agent who handled her lease quickly caught her eye. The letter, official and to the point felt heavy in her hands and a feeling of dread came over her as she read:

Dear Tenant,

We regret to inform you that following a repossession order in favour of Allied Trust Bank, the property located on 34 Main Street, Lakeview will be terminating its lease agreement with your business as of January 1 in the new year. We thank you for your cooperation at this time.

CHAPTER 9

Repossession order?

Ella's hands tremored as she dropped the letter to the ground. Her lively face drained of colour and she forcefully held back panic as she attempted to maintain a sense of calm in front of her staff and customers.

Quickly taking her cane, she departed for her small office out back. She couldn't hold her anger in anymore as she forcefully slammed her door, not caring if Colm or the other staff heard her. She needed a moment to think and to re-read in private and she did not want to be interrupted.

Ella had been aware of her lease changing

hands over time. Just two years before, she had been forced to pay almost double her old rent when Heidi's husband took over.

Now, despite the fact that Ella always paid her dues on time, it seemed like Paul had defaulted on his mortgage responsibilities and thus the bank wanted to take the property back.

It was an unimaginable, and utterly *crushing* blow.

She didn't quite understand. When Paul had taken over the building, she'd simply received a letter informing her of the change and where she should send her monthly rent payments. Why couldn't the bank just take her lease over? Why was she being thrown out? Unless the repossession order meant that the bank was planning to sell….

Her mind raced in terror. Perhaps she could afford to buy the building herself, but the thought of the price made her abandon that idea as quickly as it had come. While she had managed to scrimp and save over the years, she never had much left over except to pay for her own mortgage and utility bills.

A building like this in such a prime location

would have to be on the market for *way* more than she could ever afford.

The party suddenly came back to the forefront of her mind. Momentarily, Ella had forgotten all about Heidi's planning books and her insistence that the café celebrations be at her Lakeview mini-palace.

Did she know what her husband was up to? That he had been taking Ella's money but hadn't been keeping up repayments on the property?

She thought again about the declined credit card and wondered then if there were financial problems behind all these largesse displays. Or worse, she wondered now, did Heidi know all along that Ella was going to be thrown out and was taking pity on her by hosting the party? And was this why she seemed so distracted and evasive at the meeting earlier?

Tears began to flow from Ella's eyes as she rummaged through her desk drawers. Grabbing a dusty brown folder from the bottom of a neglected shelf, she quickly pulled out a large stack of pictures.

She had avoided looking at these for so

long, but now the pictures of her husband, father-in-law and former staff of the café down through the years were an immediate comfort. She flipped through the pictures of customers sitting at the same tables still in use today, ordering tea and coffee from the counter.

In one particularly striking picture, Ella saw her husband as a teenager mopping the very room she herself was in now. In the photo, Gregory's hair spiked and curled in a carefree way like his wide, toothy smile. His white shirt and black work pants were filthy, a trait she would later nag him about, yet he would never allow her to buy him new clothing unless they were completely destroyed.

Seeing her husband in these images calmed her, if only temporarily.

"What would you do, Gregory?" she whispered into the void, in the hope that an answer would come as easily to her.

The last photo in the stack was of the café, her beautiful sanctuary, lit up at Christmastime. The walls were adorned with sparkly tinsel, and holly and ivy decorated the display cases. In the centre of the photo stood the staff;

her husband, probably about twenty years old at the time, stood dead centre wearing a silly Santa hat. Behind him, Ella spotted a much younger version of herself wearing a velvet dress and a joyous smile.

She remembered that very day. It was Christmas Eve and the staff were just about to knock off for the night.

As they left, Gregory insisted on staying behind just a little while longer with Ella. He dimmed the lights as the last person left and spun on his heels. Then he turned and walked towards her with an ease that made her knees shake.

She had been working at the café for a few months and had developed such a crush on the owner's son. His boisterous laugh, his ease with strangers and his devotion to his family had made him quite the catch.

Despite seeing each other almost every day, they hadn't spoken very often. When he had asked her to stay behind, Ella really couldn't imagine what it would be for. But now, as he approached her, he did not have to say a word. Instead, he looked at her straight in the eye and swept a piece of chestnut hair from her forehead to behind her ear.

"Ella Ryan, I want to kiss you. Will you let me?" His question was so earnest, so sincere. It was passionate without being forceful. Ella had never been kissed before, but she nodded, speechless. He tipped her chin back and leaned his head to hers. His lips gently brushed her forehead first, then her cheek, and finally her own mouth. The sensation knocked her breath away.

And even now, all these years later, she found herself stunned, touching her lips as if that first kiss had happened to her right here and now.

Her answer to her earlier question became clear. Ella knew what she had to do. While she may not be able to save the Heartbreak Café from closing, she would be able to keep her promise to thank the town for their custom and to celebrate her husband's legacy.

She would not let all those great memories fade into the darkness with the rest of her business. She would instead throw the best celebration she could.

Steadfast and focused, she brushed her tears

from her eyes, and stored the eviction letter in her desk drawer, before heading out to the kitchen to find Colm and the crew.

Ella wasn't about to let another moment go to waste when there was so much to be done.

CHAPTER 10

A phone began to ring loudly in Ruth's ears.

She stirred but didn't roll over. She could already guess who it was and why they were calling. She looked at the digital clock next to her reading 4:07 in bright red digits, then sighed and picked up the landline.

But no, it wasn't her agent, it was one of the locals looking for Charlie.

"Hello?" she heard him say brightly as she passed him the handset. Even at this early hour, her husband was commanding and alive, unlike Ruth who could barely peel her eyes open. "I can get there in about fifteen minutes. And don't panic, I'll organise a courtesy car in the meantime."

As he hung up, she mustered enough energy to roll over and face Charlie as he quickly threw on some jeans and a flannel shirt.

"Who was that, hon?" She could barely make out the words, but she was curious and genuinely wanted to know what was so important that it would rouse her husband from bed at this unreasonable hour.

"Luke. His car is giving trouble and he needs to be in Rosslare to get the morning boat."

A more recent addition to the community, Luke worked for months on end on Atlantic oil rigs so he wouldn't want to miss the ferry to his next destination.

"Say hi to Tara for me if she's awake," she mumbled blearily, referring to Luke's girlfriend who ran a life-coaching clinic from their house.

Giving up her LA lifestyle had necessitated lots of adjustments for Ruth and in the early days, Tara had been a godsend. They were now no longer client/coach, but great friends.

"I might just drop him down to the port

altogether rather than having to mess around with paperwork for a courtesy car, especially as he'll be gone for months."

She smiled. "You're a saint, do you know that? What would this town do without you?" She meant every word. Charlie was beloved by everyone—the local hero who always went out of his way to make sure everyone in Lakeview was taken care of. She couldn't help but be in awe of his dedication.

"I'll see you later then. I'll try to drop back in the afternoon if I can. I'm going to go give Scarlett a kiss, grab an apple, and let you get back to your beauty sleep." With that, he swooped down, kissed her softly on the forehead and went across the hall to Scarlett's room.

Ruth lay in bed as she heard her husband's quick footsteps move from the bedroom, down the stairs to the kitchen, and out to the garage. When she confirmed that the car had left and the garage was safely shut, she quickly threw off her covers and headed downstairs to the living room where she had left her handbag and the script.

Mailed from her agent a few days before,

Ruth had had little time to study it properly with Charlie being in and out of the house and Scarlett demanding more and more of her. Now with the promise of some alone time, she could finally read and assess.

All she knew about the untitled movie was that her agent had called it a "once-in-a-lifetime opportunity." It was her chance to work with some of the biggest names in Hollywood, including a director who was well-known for working with former TV actors and making them megastars. His last two movies had won Academy Awards. In Ruth's hands was a script for his next big film and it seemed they were practically giving her the lead role without even an audition.

She dived right in. The movie centred around a young female factory worker who falls in love with a doomed foreman. It was a complete page-turner and Ruth hung on every word and every direction. When the characters fell in love, she did too. And when her potential part died, she burst into tears as if watching the scene come to life.

She was only brought back to reality when Scarlett appeared at the top of the stairs ready to start her day. It was 7 am and Ruth was soon back to reality.

"Hey there, sunshine! How was your night? Did you sleep well?"

"Mummy, where's Dad?" Ruth's heart melted whenever Scarlett called Charlie "dad."

"He went to work. He's had to go and save someone, but you will see him later. Right now, let's get you breakfast and then ready for creche. What do you think?" She hopped upstairs, leaving the script and note from the agent still sitting on the couch to be further read and dissected later.

By eight, Ruth and Scarlett had made it to creche just in time. While Ruth hated leaving her daughter there in the mornings, she hoped it would be the best place for her to socialise. Her daughter had opportunities to run around, meet children her own age, and learn from the preschool curriculum. The creche itself cared for almost every child in the town under the age of five, so it was also an opportunity for Ruth to meet the other mothers.

Today, there were a few different faces in the entryway.

"Morning Ruth! How is Scarlett? I heard

Charlie was out early this morning on a call." The owner, Mrs. Lane approached her politely.

"Yes. He was. It was an early morning for both Scarlett and I, so don't be surprised if she is a bit cranky." Ruth watched from the parent's viewing window as Scarlett settled into her routine.

"No worries about that. I'm sure nap time will help. Scarlett has a new classmate joining her today. Have you met Heidi? Heidi, this is Ruth Seymour. Her daughter Scarlett will be in class with Amelia."

"I don't believe I have had the pleasure," cooed a soft voice. "It's *sooo* nice to finally meet you. I have heard all about you. Of course, you're practically a legend around here!"

"Thank you, I suppose. But I'm just another Lakeview mum these days and happy to be. Your husband owns this building, doesn't he?"

"Well, um, yes. I mean I um, think so... Honestly he owns so much of this town I can't keep track," Heidi's voice was terse all of a sudden. "Anyway, I must invite you to the café Christmas party. You'll come?"

Ruth was thrown by the subject change

(and indeed this woman's involvement), but quickly caught up.

"Yes, Ella asked me to sing actually. I'm really looking forward to it. I'm rehearsing tomorrow with Nicky actually."

"That's wonderful! I don't know if you caught the address, but the party is actually being hosted at our house this time. So feel free to let me know if you have any questions about the event. It is, after all, going to be the party of the year!" As she said the words *party of the year*, Ruth could hear the strain and the nervousness in her tone. It was as if Heidi was trying to convince herself that everything was going to be as great as she made it sound.

"I'm certainly looking for — " Ruth stopped short as she noticed Heidi's attention was no longer focused on her. Instead, the woman's eyes continually darted back and forth towards the front door where other mothers were gathering. She looked as though she was on the run and needed a place to hide.

"I'm sorry, but I need to go check on my daughter. I'll see you at the party, then?" Heidi's voice was rushed and forced. She didn't even attempt to smile or lift her gaze at Ruth. Instead, she kept her focus on that door and the steady stream of women and children entering and exiting.

"Yes, see you there." With that, Ruth watched as Heidi ducked into the classroom and out of eyesight.

Within seconds of Heidi's hasty departure, Ruth was being fussed over by the group of Lakeview mums. Some she knew from school, like Nina and of course her next-door neighbour Gemma, but others were usually a blur to her.

All of them knew her though, her husband, and her reputation. There was always incessant chatter about their favourite episodes, handsome co-actors and award show gossip. Ruth attempted to keep up most of the time, but these ladies seemed to know more about her old life than she did.

These discussions merely highlighted how far away from that life she was now. Growing up, dreaming of becoming a star, it was all she ever wanted—to be recognised, admired, and fawned over.

But now that she was back in Lakeview, it felt less significant. A part of her yearned to be back in the business so that she could be more than just a has-been and community gossip fodder.

After tangling with the creche mothers, Ruth needed a pick me up, and Ella's coffee and breakfast pastries were the only cure she could think of to get over her Hollywood homesick blues. But Ruth had learnt her lesson last time. Before she entered the café, she quickly surveyed it from her car for any signs of her mother-in-law. If Ita was inside, she'd have to do without.

Luckily for her, there was no sign.

In fact, there wasn't a single soul in the café—a first for that hour of the morning that Ruth could recall. Tables were empty and counter stools appeared to not have been used since the day before. The staff was at a minimum. If there were tumbleweeds in Lakeview, they would have stopped here.

Ruth seated herself at the counter while she waited for someone to appear. From the back, Ella quietly approached her. Unlike her usual, bubbly self, today she seemed aloof and almost pensive. It was a bit disarming given that part of the café's enduring appeal was Ella's bright smile and hospitality.

"Hello, Ruth. What can I get for you?" Her voice was soft and meek and Ruth could sense that she was tense and absent, even. Maybe the party arrangements were taking their toll on her or more likely, perhaps Queen Bee Heidi was taking a toll.

"Just a skinny latte and a Danish, if you have any." Ruth eyed the surprisingly sparse display counter.

"I'll check. In the meantime, I'm just letting every customer know that December 21st will be our last day in business."

"What?" Ruth was massively taken aback. This news was totally out of left field. Ella's café was an institution. There was no way she wasn't doing enough business to keep the place afloat. "Ella, what on earth's happened? Why are you closing? Is there anything I can do?"

"Ah no, pet. It's just time for me to...ah... retire. This café has been my life for too long. I'm letting it go now."

"Isn't there someone who could take over

for you and keep this place alive? Surely Colm would jump at the chance?" Ruth felt herself intruding but she was still in shock from the news itself.

"No, pet. He has his own plans. Anyway, let me go and get you that Danish."

Ruth sat at the empty counter looking at her hands.

It was strange to think of the word 'retirement' where Ella was concerned. To Ruth's limited knowledge, her adult children all lived away. Yes, she had her stray animals but what would she do if she retired? Why would she sacrifice doing something that she loved so much to just make do with a bunch of cats and dogs?

The word 'sacrifice' echoed through Ruth's mind and instantly reminded her of that script sitting on the couch back home, and the decision that she herself would soon need to make.

She had never been one to settle for anything but her dreams. So why now when Scarlett was old enough was she still sacrificing her career? Her mind raced with regret and dare she say it, remorse for all the things she herself had given up.

Ella reappeared with the coffee and pastry.

"You look like you have something on your mind, honey." She broke the silence between the two as she passed Ruth the white plate and red cup.

"I was just thinking about retirement. It must have been a hard decision, but you're probably feeling good about it too?"

"Sometimes you have to make the hard decisions. Life is full of them. But once you know what your gut is saying, you have to just go for it. Head first. Even if it hurts or feels helpless, when it is time, it is time."

Ruth studied Ella's face. Her eyes had those soft, wave-like wrinkles around her eyes and her hands were cracked—most likely from washing dishes and serving customers for over thirty years. This woman had devoted her life to her work, the work that she loved. While Ella Harris may have seemed tired, passion still radiated off of her in waves.

"You know what, I think I am going to take these to go," Ruth told her. "I have some calls to make and I probably should get to it." She quickly grabbed her coat from the back of her chair, paid Ella and darted outside onto Main

Street, her coffee spilling carelessly as she sped to her parked car.

She knew what she had to do.

Hollywood was once again calling and Ruth needed to decide once and for all whether or not she would answer.

CHAPTER 11

"I've been laid off."

Heidi stared across the kitchen table at Paul.

"What do you mean *laid off*? When? Is this a joke, like that thing with the credit card? If it is, it isn't very funny and I do not appreciate being teased."

Her husband just stared at his plate in silence.

"Oh Paul," Heidi lamented, trying to think back to anything that could have pointed to this coming. Was it the regional manager's visit that he had obsessed about? Maybe it was the closures of other branches throughout the city. He had talked constantly about how all these huge changes in the banking industry would eventually mean lay-offs and redundancies.

"They just didn't need me anymore," he said stoically. "I don't think there was anything I could have done or said." He seemed resolved but uncharacteristically quiet. She barely recognised the man who was so often full of life and laughter.

"How could they not need you? You're an area manager. You've been at that bank since you were twenty-one. This is ridiculous, Paul. It really is."

"There's more." His voice lowered and his head still pointed downward as he avoided eye contact with her. He reminded Heidi of a scolded dog or one who knew that he was about to get in trouble. "We're in a lot of debt."

"Well we will just have to find you a new job of course," Heidi continued, as if he hadn't spoken. "Our savings will hold us over until you find another, better-paying position." Her voice changed to optimism. She needed to believe it, for her own sake.

"That's the thing, babe, there are no savings. We used our savings to buy all the rental properties but it seems I leveraged them too high to keep up all the repayments and ... bottom line is the bank is repossessing everything." He met her gaze. "And I mean everything."

"Repossessing what? The rental properties?" His silence then led her to a stark realisation. "The house, *this* house too? No, Paul! Not our home! Amelia has lived here since birth. We have raised her here. We have made a home here. I will not part with this place."

"Honey, I'm sorry. I really am. But I've been looking at the numbers for a while now so if we truly want to hold onto this place, we have to make serious cuts — and fast. Miriam has to go. The renovations are off. We're going to have to think about selling a car or two in the meantime just to make the next repayment. I've been trying to keep things going for as long as I could by using rental income from the investment properties to pay off this place, but with the layoff ... I'm not sure what to do now."

"You can't be serious!" This house was Heidi's crowning glory. It was everything she had ever wanted. Now that, along with their entire lives, was under threat. And all the rental properties in their hometown to be repossessed? She couldn't stand it.

"Listen," he said tentatively, "one of my old golfing buddies has been interested in this place for years. When I was let go, he approached me and asked me about it again. Maybe we should consider selling. The equity would hold us over for a while at least."

"Paul, no, please! Think of Amelia. We cannot do this to her. We cannot do this to *us*. We have to make things work without selling the house." She pleaded with him, her voice breaking as tears pooled in her eyes.

"Like I said, I've tried everything and there is nothing else we can do. We're behind on all the rentals and if we can't make the next mortgage repayment, which we can't with none of us working, the house will eventually have to be sold anyway. We have to let Miriam go straight away. If we don't get a handle on things, we will not be able to stay on top of our bills for much more than two or three weeks with my redundancy package." His voice was firm. This was it. He needed to tell Heidi that. He needed to make her know that this was the only way.

"I just don't understand." As she sat in their beautiful kitchen, her husband gently kissed the top of her forehead, brushed the hair out of her face and turned to leave.

"I know you don't." His resolve melted into what Heidi could only describe as guilt. It looked like it was overwhelming him. "I am sorry that I cannot make this right for you, sweetheart. All that I have ever wanted was to give you and Amelia the world and I failed you. I am never going to stop being sorry about that. But you have to know that if there was any other way, I would have found it. It just ... is what it is."

"I know ..." Her voice quivered as she struggled to find an answer to his world-rocking confession. But Heidi had no other words. She had no way to express her true feelings without making it worse for him. This was going to have to be her battle. It would be too much to make Paul feel even more guilt that he didn't deserve.

He quietly left for his study, closing the grand French doors behind him. She listened to his soft and slow footsteps as he walked to his leather lounge chair, a chair that had belonged to his father years before. He turned on the room's 40-inch flatscreen television, lowered the volume and faded into the background.

Upstairs, Amelia was already in bed asleep. The long day of creche and then play with the nanny had worn her out, and she quickly fell asleep soon after Paul had come home from work. For the first time since her daughter was born, Heidi was grateful for the silence. While she had spent every moment thankful for the laughter, the shrieks, the cries, and even the occasional tantrum, having this moment alone to process everything was a gift.

Heidi got up to clear her and Paul's plates and the dinner dishes. As she passed the patio doors, the view of her back garden came into view. All those barbecue and garden party memories, with Paul on the grill, Amelia in her arms and friends and family gathered around, came flooding back like a cruel joke.

This was not the time to be nostalgic though, Heidi decided. This was her reality. This was her *life*. She had to accept it one way or another. Paul knew what he was talking about and if he said this house might have to be sold, then it might have to be sold. There was no use trying to deny it.

The helplessness broke her down. It crumbled her heart and dulled her mind. She went about the housework mindlessly. She picked up Amelia's toys from the living room, cleaned the kitchen countertops and tried to hum along to a song on her radio as she prepared her clothing and accessories for tomorrow.

Tomorrow, she told herself, channelling Scarlett O'Hara, one of her favourite movie heroines, *I will awake from this nightmare. I just have to get through tonight. Tomorrow will be better and brighter. Tomorrow will be OK.*

CHAPTER 12

When Heidi awoke at six the following morning, Paul was already gone. It was a familiar sight. She rarely woke up to him still being home unless it was a rare day off or he was sick. He had always strived to be first in the office long before his subordinates arrived.

His absence when she awoke gave her a bit of a jolt. *Maybe last night really* didn't *happen*, she thought to herself. She sprang out of bed, grabbed her robe and headed to the bathroom in hopes of starting her day on the right foot.

When she came out to get dressed, the familiar voice of her husband coming from the hallway crept in through the half-open door.

"I am so sorry Miriam. We never wanted this to happen. We never even saw it coming."

"I understand. I really do."

"As soon as we can hire you back, we will. We just don't know when that will be."

"I will really miss little Amelia." Heidi could hear Miriam fighting back a sob as she said her charge's name out loud.

"Please feel free to stay here as long as you need to."

Or at least for as long as we're allowed to keep this place, Heidi thought mournfully.

"That's not necessary but thank you. I can stay with my sister in Dublin until I find myself another placement. Would you be comfortable with writing me a letter of recommendation?"

"Certainly. If there is anything at all you need, just let Heidi or I know."

"How is she doing? Is she taking the news okay?"

Heidi yearned to run down the stairs and hug Miriam. How lovely that instead of focusing on her ending job, the girl seemed to genuinely care about how Heidi was handling the big news. She wished she had appreciated her more.

"Not well, I'm afraid." Paul's voice had become a whisper as if he suspected Heidi could hear him. "She cried in her sleep last night. I knew it was going to be tough, but I could never imagine it would break her this much."

"I'm sure she will recover soon. Your wife is strong-willed but always manages to land on her feet. Don't count her out."

"Thanks, Miriam. Again, if you need anything…" His voice trailed off as they moved from the downstairs living room into another part of the house.

Reality again hit Heidi like a ton of bricks. This was her new life.

No nanny. No cleaner. No manicures. No trips to Dublin to high-end stores. She made a mental list of everything she would need to get done immediately, from cancelling her next hair appointment to rescheduling the Lakeview Mum's Club meeting.

She would also have to return the expensive Christmas gifts she had purchased—the watch and ties for Paul and the endless amount of clothing and toys for Amelia. And all her new clothes too of course, including the beautiful

Dolce & Gabbana dress she'd planned to wear for the big Christmas shindig.

The thought of Christmas without gifts or maybe even a home rattled her to the core. Being bankrupt was not how she had envisioned it. Luckily, Amelia would still be young enough to forget. Years from now she wouldn't remember the lack of a tree or the missing presents. She would have no idea about the un-RSVP'd parties.

Ella's party came again to Heidi's mind. Amidst all this new stress, she had forgotten about her promise about hosting it and her meetings with Ella where she had discussed decorative choices and how everything would be staged. All of that seemed like a million years ago now.

But suddenly, it dawned on her: Paul had been talking about the rental properties being repossessed. One of those properties was the very building in which the café was housed, wasn't it?

Dread racing through her mind, Heidi hurtled down the stairs and into her husband's study.

He sat at his imposing, wooden desk

looking over his stacks of paperwork. As she entered, he barely looked up at her or acknowledged her presence.

"Paul!" she cried breathlessly. "Are you closing down the café?"

"What? What are you talking about?" He studied her quizzically. She had never asked about his business in the past and rarely showed interest in the properties he picked up or the stocks he chose, other than to boast about them of course.

"The properties the bank wants to take. Is one of them The Heartbreak Café?"

"The what?" he asked, still wildly confused.

"You know, Ella's place," she clarified. "Is it part of the repossession order?"

Paul looked down at his paperwork and shuffled through a pile. At the bottom of the stack, he pulled out a cream-coloured, official-looking envelope and handed it to her.

"Yes, Heidi. The café building is being repossessed too. I'm sorry."

CHAPTER 13

For Ella, the days after receiving the eviction notice were the hardest.

In the midst of attempting to plan the Christmas party with little help from a suddenly absent Heidi, she also had to mourn the loss of her business privately.

She could not bear to break the bad news to her staff, all of whom were depending on her to get them through the expensive holiday period. She would have to keep the news to herself until she could find an appropriate moment to tell the others.

So Ella made a plan. While her staff discussed preparing the menus for the party and serving their regular customers, she decided to plant the idea that she was nearing retirement. That way, she would feel less of a failure and more like this was coming anyway.

The idea of retirement would be a softer blow than forceful closure. At least then it was in her power and not at the mercy of some banker.

It had started with an innocent remark to Colm as they set about baking batches of snowman-shaped shortbread cookies that would be offered at the party.

"I'll tell you one thing: I will not miss *this*," she commented dourly.

"Miss what?" Colm didn't even look up from his work.

"Ah, you know," she said, pointing towards the ovens. "The same thing over and over again, day after day. When I retire, I plan on having others bake me goodies." She attempted to make herself sound exasperated.

In truth, she loved the baking process. She relished combining ingredients, preheating the oven, the scent of fresh dough and the occasional taste of creamy batter.

It reminded her of her first days back in the

old kitchen with her father-in-law teaching her the ins and outs of baked goods. And of her husband and his insistence that he try the first of everything she made.

As difficult as it was for her to lie to her staff, it was even harder to deceive some of her favourite customers.

One by one, she would casually mention her upcoming plans. It started with Ita Mellon, who was a notorious gossip. She knew that if Ita caught on to her 'retirement', the rest of the town would be in talks of it by the end of the week.

"Ita," she'd casually interjected as she poured her friend another cup of coffee, "Do you know of anyone around here who works in finding post-retirement activities?"

"Here, in Lakeview?" Ita's wheels were slowly turning, Ella could tell by the gleam in her eye and the urgency in her tone. "Other than golfing, I doubt it. The way we treat our senior citizens these da—"

"No, I'm not interested in golf. Maybe volunteering or something like that. In any case, I need to do something to entertain myself once I finish up here."

"I suppose so..." Ita was looking at Ella and her voice now had an excited shake as if she'd been handed a secret key. No doubt she was already making a mental note of who in the town to break the news to first.

As Ita left in her haste, Ella realised that this was the beginning of the end. This was how her retirement started. That word stung the more and more she thought of it. Her father-in-law would have never retired. Her husband definitely would have put his foot down at the very thought too. Ella attempted to swallow back the disappointment at herself. But this was her only option, wasn't it?

Come noon, the café had emptied. The place was uncharacteristically quiet for lunchtime. The only customers so far that morning had been Ruth Seymour, a few passing tourists and a couple of the local teenagers sneaking out of school for an early lunch run.

Ella went back to help Colm prepare afternoon pastries, yet she had a feeling that the rest of the day would also be atypically quiet.

Her ruse must have done the trick. Of course, word had spread like wildfire. Ita wouldn't be able to resist telling everyone she ran into. No doubt she had stopped into Rich Rags, the boutique up the road, the hair salon and several houses of her friends and neighbours. By now, she estimated that at least half the town had received word that Ella was retiring.

In the quiet and the calm, she went out back to her office beside the kitchen as Colm quietly chatted and went about his day, none the wiser. She should start packing things up, she told herself, but she instead decided to sort through the stacks of invoices and bills, timesheets and staff notes and the couple of random menu mockups she had begun to compose for January.

She began to tear through the pile like a madwoman on a mission. Her rubbish bin filled up quickly with the bits of pieces she found disposable. Within minutes, her tiny workstation was completely clear of familiar and comforting clutter.

All that was left to do was to make a moving-out list. There would be equipment to sell, things to move and staff to let go. It all felt so overwhelming and daunting, yet she knew she couldn't ignore it for long. Christmas was less than two weeks away and then she would have only another few days throughout the holiday period to get the place clear and empty in time for the end.

As her list began to add up, a knock came at the door. It was urgent, forceful and familiar. Colm typically let himself in but this person insisted on knocking.

Wiping her eyes and clearing mascara streaks from her face, Ella replied: "Come in." She kept her back facing the door.

"Ella, when were you going to tell me?" The voice was firm, yet soothing. She swivelled in her desk chair, meeting Joseph's eyes. Without speaking a word, she stared at him for a few seconds. He looked tired and worn. She couldn't imagine how she appeared at that moment to him. She couldn't do more than stare into his icy blue irises and study the way his greying hair shone in the desk light. Goodness, he was a handsome man.

He in return couldn't help but survey Ella and the way that she looked small and wounded. Her cast was still on, her body bent over the desk, and her pile of paperwork was carelessly tossed in the bin next to her. He wanted nothing more than to kneel down next to her and hold her hand.

"I'm so sorry." Despite herself, Ella began to sob. She had forgotten to tell him. She had forgotten that her old friend and most loyal customer should know first. Not that he needed to, but she had wanted to. She had wanted to tell Joseph everything.

With her cries, he moved across to her, gently placing one arm on the top of her heaving back, as the other grabbed the chair next to her. He sat down quickly, facing her directly. His hand casually rubbed her shoulders and her neck.

"Ella, pet. Please, please stop crying. Let's just talk. Just tell me what you are thinking, what you are doing."

"What I am doing? I am not doing anything!" Her outburst took him aback. He had never seen her act this way. He felt as if he should spring into action, yet she was giving him no direction.

"But, I heard you were retiring and closing down the café. Is that true? If it is, it's okay….

it's exciting even. A big step but you would probably lo—"

"No, Joseph, I'm not retiring. I'm being evicted." Ella hadn't planned on telling anyone the truth, yet here she was confessing all. Maybe it was the way he touched her tenderly or how he faced her head-on. She couldn't help herself as she went on to explain how she received the estate agent's letter and had no other option but to clear out.

And how she had lied to Ita and Colm to soften the blow.

"Why couldn't you tell everyone the truth? Maybe it would help you keep the café?"

"I just couldn't. Look at me. I don't ask for help. I *give* help. For thirty years I have helped people in this town find jobs, mind their children, sort through their marriage problems, and take in their abandoned animals. Yet I wouldn't dream of asking a thing of anyone. Gregory would have never let me ask for help. He always said "Our problems are *our* problems.'"

Until she had said this, she had forgotten that her husband had always lived by the unwritten rule that those who stepped into the café were allowed to share their problems, while those working in it would keep theirs private. It kept up a mystique and the charm.

"You cannot live your life like that. I know that you want to keep this place. I know that you would never, ever retire—much less go take up *golfing*."

He was right of course—but that didn't change her resolve. "This is how it is, Joseph. This is how it has to be. It breaks my heart to have to close but I have no choice. The Heartbreak Café is finally living up to its nickname."

Just as he was so certain that he knew her well enough to keep her from giving up this place, Ella was equally certain that she had to.

"Come on. Let's just talk this through. You could talk to the estate agent and find out if the bank might let you stay on as a sitting tenant or something. We can come up with a plan." His genuine desire to help was admirable, but Ella knew better.

She shook her head. "There is no 'we' in this Joseph. This is *my* café, and *I* will decide how I want this to end." She looked away from him, not daring to meet his gaze, which she knew would be wounded by her stalwart rejection.

"I'm sorry, but I need to get back out there now. The afternoon crowd should be coming through and I am a bit short-staffed." She slowly stood, her weight leaning onto her stick.

He stood too, towering over her.

"I'm sorry. I didn't mean to imply anything. I just want to help you. Make sure that you are OK and that this is what you really want?"

"What I really want is to get out there and serve my customers while I still have any. Are you staying?" She couldn't help but offer some hospitality for his troubles, but by the way he looked at her, she could sense that Joseph was hurt.

"No. I'd better get back to work myself. I will see you tomorrow though. And the next day. And the next. I will be here till the very end or until you ask me to leave."

He stared down at her as he placed his hand on her cheek and rubbed his rough thumb over where her face had turned a glowing pink. Using the tip of his finger, he brushed a tear from the tip of her eye. And without a word more, Joseph opened the door and walked back out.

Ella stood in the dark corner of her office

touching the place where his hand had been. She hadn't been touched there by anyone else in years. It was so personal and intimate that it took her several moments to recover. But in those passing seconds, she realised something else deep and real.

For the first time in decades, Ella Harris thought she might be falling in love.

CHAPTER 14

That afternoon, things did pick up substantially at the café. A busload of tourists arrived and a steady stream of locals came in to offer their personal opinions regarding Ella's retirement.

"We will so miss you and your amazing quiches!"

"Will you stay in town?"

"Will Colm be taking over the café? He'd be great, but I don't know if he has your business sense."

"Who is going to take care of the catering for our parties now?"

The last comment came from the village queen bee herself, Cynthia Roland. Since she was a young child, Cynthia had basically taken over the place with her know-it-all smirks and her insistence that she knew everything about everyone. In comparison, Cynthia made Ita's gossipy and judgemental tendencies look like child's play.

Today, she was joined by the group of women who called themselves the Lakeview Mum's Club, but whom Ella had more often heard referred to as 'The Mummy Martyrs'.

Flanking both sides of Cynthia, they travelled in packs with their strollers and baby carriers. Each carried a designer nappy bag in their designated colour, a fresh bottle or dummy - and a nasty attitude.

Times had not changed much from when these women were in school and their accessories were backpacks, makeup cases and an unsuspecting boyfriend from the football team. Now all married to successful men working in Dublin, the girls had no other purpose than to rule Lakeview with an iron fist.

They dictated everything from what hairstyle was de rigeur at the beauty salon, which cocktail was in vogue and which boutique was a must for the latest fashions. Dare to contradict them or refuse to play nice to their demands, and there would be consequences.

Their refusal to shop in certain places in town had closed several new businesses down. Ella knew it was a delicate balance, so she either played along or avoided them altogether. The drama, in her opinion, was way beneath her. But today, there was no other staff to take their order or to set up high chairs for their crying, snotty children. It was all on Ella to make sure their needs were met to their impeccable standards.

She seated the group in the front section of tables closest to the window, but more importantly far enough away from the other customers. The women preferred it this way. They could chat loudly while watching and judging the townspeople passing by the windows. Their children, on the other hand, could be supervised by Ella as she worked the counter and checked out customers from the front.

"It's such as shame about this place. It was always so … what is the word, um … charming." Deirdre piped up first, ignoring the fussy baby to her right as he attempted to grab the ketchup bottle next to him.

"I agree, but what can you do to stop progress?" Emer was practically salivating at the thought of a coffee giant moving in. "I'm hopeful that we'll finally get that Starbucks this place desperately needs."

"Well I for one, will be glad of an upgrade," Cynthia agreed. "This town needs to get with the times. No more run-down takeaways or discount grocers." She wrinkled her nose. "With the closing of this place, I can see the whole Main Street changing for the better."

Of course, Cynthia had to own the idea that what the town needed was big businesses turfing out what had been in place for years before her time as queen bee.

"Hear, hear!" Emer laughed loudly as she agreed with Cynthia's proclamation. The whole group cackled together as they discussed popular chains that should replace some of the older shops on the street.

Not a single stone was left unturned, or any business left unscathed as Deirdre even took notes on the girl's opinions as if she were the acting secretary of a select town meeting.

After several minutes, Ella headed over to take their orders. As she passed by the door, a hooded figure entered quietly with eyes focused straight ahead. The two collided, with Ella stumbling a bit. The other person caught her, giving Ella a chance to realise who she had run into.

"Oh, I'm sorry Heidi! I didn't see you coming in." She hadn't recognised her either with her face concealed in an oversized sweatshirt that almost certainly belonged to her husband. From what Ella could tell, she was makeup-free and her hair had been hastily gathered in a messy bun at the top of her head.

"Are you OK?" Heidi whispered with her head deliberately turned away from the window, but Ella wasn't sure if she was referring to their brief collision or the fact that her husband's financial carelessness was putting her out of business.

"I'm fine. Just getting used to this cane. Why don't you take a seat wherever you can find one, and I'll bring you a fresh cup of coffee."

Heidi quickly shuffled herself to the back, finally settling on a place near the end of the counter. Her back was turned as she studied a menu.

Ella returned to the girls' table with pen and paper ready for their orders, but they were too distracted by the new entry to pay her any heed.

"Is *that* who I think it is? Gemma, is that her?" Emer ducked in towards the table's centre with her finger pointed directly at Heidi's back.

"I'm not sure. It's hard to tell without the nanny following her every move," Gemma whispered.

"Who does she think she is? That girl has no class." Cynthia refused to keep her voice down like the rest of them. She said it loud enough for everyone in the surrounding area to hear. "You think that her husband going bankrupt would make her a humbler person. Yet it seems as if her money was the only thing forcing her to play nice." All but one of the women nodded solemnly at this seemingly deft observation.

"I heard they never had all the money they claimed to in the first place. The reason Paul was fired from the bank was because she put them into so much debt with her spending."

"That's not true, Deirdre. It's because Paul was caught stealing money, probably so that Heidi could spend, spend, spend on that spoiled little brat of hers," Emer was going straight for the jugular.

"Gemma, is it true that they've already sold the house?" Cynthia sat up straight at the thought of fresh news to add to Heidi's tales of woe.

"Not yet. Paul says they're trying to hold on to it."

"But if they have to sell the house, where will they move to? Certainly not to our estate, I hope." Deirdre sounded absolutely frightened at the prospect of a bankrupt family moving in across the road.

"No, but I think they are looking for something smaller, maybe an apartment."

"An *APARTMENT!*" Cynthia laughed maniacally at the thought of Heidi downgrading. The rest of the girls joined in, their laughter overtaking the conversations of the other diners who were not already eavesdropping. All but Heidi had turned to pay attention.

"I think that's enough, Cynthia." Ella made

her presence known as she tapped the well-coiffed woman on the shoulder.

"Excuse me?" Cynthia seemed genuinely shocked.

"I am politely asking you to keep your voices down so as not to disturb the other diners. We all just want to enjoy our food in peace." Ella stared daggers at the rest of the women. She was one hundred percent serious about her command.

"Well, oh dear. It looks as if we have disturbed the rest of the customers, what few you have." The other woman's voice oozed with sarcasm and disregard. "OK, we promise that we will keep our voices down, Ella." She batted her eyes innocently at the café owner. The rest of the women snickered.

"Cynthia Roland, I have known you since you were a small child and while I have refused to step in before, I am saying this now—you are no longer welcome in this establishment. If you cannot respect my wishes or indeed the lives of the other, respectable customers, then you will not be served here. Do I make myself clear?"

The girls stared wordlessly at one another.

One of their babies began to cry, but the mums continued to ignore her. All eyes were placed squarely on Ella and back at Cynthia.

The rest of the café seemed to have leaned in to see what would happen next. You could hear a pin drop.

"Well, ladies, it looks like we will take our business elsewhere. This café has long lost all appeal to me anyway. Perhaps it's good that the place be gutted and replaced by something more civilised."

Ella's heart burst in anger. "You four wouldn't know civilised if it slapped you in the face. I recommend that you leave now before I call Colm to escort you and your ill-behaved cohort out this door."

With that, Ella turned, picked up the coffee pot and proceeded to serve the rest of the customers who had sat in silence—some with their mouths gaping open.

The group duly left without another word, slamming the door behind them. Ella watched from the corner of her eye as they struggled with their pushchairs and their fussy, irritable children. In front of the café window, they remained each loudly debating about what had just happened.

Cynthia, in a rage, fled first away from the group and Julia followed suit, running to keep up with her. Emer hesitated for a bit but eventually followed in a quick step.

Gemma stayed behind. With her toddler in her arms, she glanced back into the café as if she wanted to come back inside. Yet, after a few seconds of hesitation, she picked up her nappy bag from the ground and headed towards the lakeside car park where the women had parked their identical cars. Her head hung low as she disappeared out of sight.

The café remained silent for several minutes. All were looking to Ella to make a move or to say something else. In the air was a mix of fear, respect, and wonder.

Ella hated it. She had never kicked anyone out of her café before, and now with her final weeks upon her, she had made the place inhospitable. But while she wanted to feel ashamed at how childishly she'd handled the situation, she couldn't help but give herself a pat on the back for standing up to the bullish women too.

After all, what harm could they do to her now?

She began to circle through the café. At each table, she greeted those she had yet to say hello to and listened respectfully as each gave their regards about her retirement. She chose to give hugs, free coffee and kind smiles to those who seemed genuinely shaken by the loss of her business. This was the side of the community that she had loved and adored all these years.

As she reached the end of the tables, she could not help but notice that Heidi remained at the counter. One of the waiting staff had served her a cup of tea and a ham sandwich. Yet, she had barely touched her food or her drink. Instead, she kept her eyes towards the back of the room, away from the rest of the prying town that had overheard what the others had said about her and her husband.

Ella took a deep breath. While the last thing she wanted to do was chat with Heidi Clancy, she knew that she couldn't just ignore her any longer. She could not avoid the situation.

Circling the counter, she could instantly tell that the younger woman had been crying. Her eyes were muddy and her face had streaks from where the tears had flowed. Ella handed her several napkins to which she silently dabbed at her cheeks.

"Heidi pet, I think it's about time you and I talked about what's going on with our party."

CHAPTER 15

Heidi had heard almost every word uttered by her 'friends', but it was nothing compared to what she had already suffered through.

For several days, talk had spread like wildfire throughout the town of her husband's job loss and their bankruptcy. Vultures had practically lined up to take shots at the formerly affluent family that was now reduced to pieces.

While Heidi had done her best to avoid the crowds, the gazers and the gossip (and even her own family), still it followed her everywhere. Whether she was dropping her daughter off at creche or picking up detergent from the local corner shop, there was always someone whispering in a corner about what had happened to them.

Even poor Amelia wasn't immune. Just yesterday, she had asked Heidi why Daddy was at home in the afternoon. When Heidi explained that Paul was trying to get a new job and that this was a little 'holiday' for the three of them, Heidi's two-year-old began to use the word *fired* as if it was just something she knew had happened.

Nothing was more heartbreaking than realising your toddler had to be a witness to other's insensitivities. Heidi couldn't take it anymore, so she took Amelia out, away from prying eyes and cruel mouths. Amelia's new childminder was Paul, who looked after her as he sent out CVs and made calls to old business associates.

Meanwhile, she had taken it upon herself to handle everything else in order to shield Paul from some of the village talk. She picked up boxes from the hardware shop, sold her beloved clothes and shoes at a designer exchange in Dublin and occasionally stopped in for groceries at Tesco. She listened to the rumours, the backhanded comments and the laughs, so she could try and protect the two people she loved from being exposed to it.

But what had happened at Ella's just now was beyond compare. While most locals attempted to hide their contempt for Heidi and her family's situation, these women, including Paul's own sister, seemed to be openly rejoicing at their terrible situation.

It made her sick to think that just a few weeks ago, she was sitting in their homes, playing with their children, feeding them snacks and goodies. Heidi was once a part of that group of women and now she was abandoned and smeared as if their history never mattered.

However, as much as Heidi wanted to be mad at the rest of her former friends, she had realised early on that much of the town's maliciousness was perhaps her own doing. For all of these years, she had cultivated this character, this facade of a woman who had everything she could ever ask or desire.

She put herself on a lone pedestal for all those to admire. Who wouldn't blame these people for looking down on her when she faltered and failed? Who could stop them from feeling no remorse for the person who refused to share their good fortune and wealth but instead kept to their mansion on the hill?

Heidi had even gone so far as to lie and cheat her way there and Ella was her most recent victim. She shouldn't have presumed to host the Christmas party at her house, especially now that there may no longer even be a house.

Now, face to face with Ella herself for the first time since word was out about her family's affairs, she felt the swell of regret and remorse. Here was a woman who just defended her honour to a group of customers who practically ran this town, yet Heidi had nothing to show her gratitude.

She had nothing to give the one woman who had the nerve to put an end to the cruel comments and incessant laughter.

She was barely paying attention when Ella came over and gently touched her elbow. "We can go back to my office if you want to get out of here."

Heidi could see that Ella was also upset, but she instantly realised that this woman actually felt bad enough for her to offer some more kindness. She sighed and nodded as she blew her nose into a napkin.

Removing her hood, she followed Ella to the back of the kitchen where Colm and the other staff worked. The mood around her was sombre, but occasionally, someone cracked a joke and the group would laugh together. It felt like family; it felt like a home.

Ella unlocked the office door, turned on the lamp in the corner and pulled her desk chair next to the only empty one. The office was all wooden, almost like a den.

No doubt that this office once belonged to Ella's husband. It had that feel of a man's touch. The vintage, worn desk had to be original as well. Ella had obviously wanted to keep as much of her family as she could in this place.

Heidi realised that she had never really known much about Ella's situation. She heard several years ago that the café had once belonged to Ella's father-in-law and when he passed away, she and her husband had kept it going.

However, Ella's husband died several years later, leaving her all alone to run the place. Heidi had never confirmed this and was not about to broach the subject now, but she felt the guilt of not knowing this woman who had given her so much hospitality and loyalty better than what she had.

And now her husband's financial mismanagement was about to take it all away from her. Just when she was about to celebrate her thirtieth year in business.

"Well, I think we are going to need to make some changes to our plans for the Christmas party in light of both our new circumstances, don't you?" Ella began, obviously wanting to be in control. It was a complete change from their other meetings when Ella would sit back and listen to Heidi ramble on about her opinions and choices.

"Yes," she mustered. "I think that'll be necessary."

"Let's start with the basics—venue first. I think we are going to have to move the party back here to the café. Space isn't a concern and seeing how today is going, I am guessing that some may be avoiding the party altogether. Not that it will be much of a loss to us…" She winked at Heidi. Even in this awkward situation, Ella was there with a bit of a joke and some charm to boot. "But the good news is and I suspect you have heard, I will be retiring at Christmas and will be closing the café for good." She emphasised the word "retiring" enough so that Heidi quickly caught on. "I will need to get rid of the furniture, the counter and much of the decor and kitchen items in anticipation. With that, there will be much more space available for folks to mingle and chat."

Heidi nodded in agreement. She couldn't help but wonder why Ella wasn't angry at her for the café shutting down. Surely she knew her family was behind it's demise?

"So while I am moving the party back here, I still need you, Heidi. I need help coordinating the music, the decorations, and the food. I will also need someone to help spread the word about the changes to the invitations. Can you do this? I mean, do you still *want* to do this?"

"Yes, I do. Of course I want to help you. I want to make this party the best this town has seen in years." She was earnest in her response because she knew she owed it to Ella to make this party exactly as she had wanted. If that meant putting herself out there to the rest of the town, Heidi would be happy to take whatever flack may come her way from the busybodies and the judgemental gossips. This she would do in service of Ella.

"Well, Colm has planned the menu, we have already started baking and now I will just need help deciding on decor. You're the best at this. What do you think?"

Heidi was taken aback by Ella and her kindness in still letting her be involved in the planning, considering. But she was more than grateful to be of any kind of help. It was the very least she could do.

"Well, we're not having much of a Christmas this year, so I can certainly bring our house decorations. I have string lights, ornaments, trees of all shapes and sizes, tinsel, Santas—table decorations, you name it, I probably have it."

"Great. I think that would be lovely and I will leave it up to your taste to decorate. I should be mostly all moved out by the twenty-first …" Heidi noticed the slight break in her voice as she said this and her heart ached for the woman, "so you will have all day before the party to work your magic. That sound OK to you?"

Heidi was speechless. Ella had given her back some of her dignity and pride. She was happy to help for as long as she would let her.

"Given the size of the room, I say we limit the music to just a keyboard and a singer. I hear that you asked Ruth to sing?"

"Yes, I think that would be an excellent idea. A band would be too loud and imposing in this space." Ella lit up at the thought of a more intimate affair, just as her husband and father-in-law had intended all those years ago.

The two continued to go through their mental to-do lists. Ella had taken out a notepad to make notes about their decisions as the two plotted and chatted about everything; from keeping Ita Mellon away from the mulled wine to how they could best space out the guests' arrival so it wouldn't get too crowded.

"What about Santa? You said we were going to organise one to call in at the end of the night." Ella's face dropped a bit then, but Heidi could not sense why. Was this another sore spot?

"I had a friend who was going to play Santa, but I am not sure if he is up to it anymore."

"Who is it? I can check with him myself if you'd like."

"No, no don't worry about that. I will talk to him. If not, there just won't be a Santa at the party, but that's okay." Ella's voice was tinged with a different kind of regret that Heidi couldn't quite understand. But she resisted prying. The old Heidi would demand to know why this person would be so flaky about such a huge responsibility. The new Heidi wanted to respect Ella's personal life as she had respected her own.

With that, the two women stood, finished with their party planning. They both looked at each other for several seconds until Heidi made the move. She stepped closer to Ella and put her arms around her in a hug. Warmth radiated off the older woman and onto Heidi. Eventually, Ella reciprocated, holding her gently with the arm not holding on to the cane.

"Thank you," Heidi said, her voice trembling. She felt herself move into the hug, almost as if her body had a mind of its own. "Thank you for everything. I'm so sorry for what has happened. Paul was stupid and neither of us ever imagined…"

"Forget it, please," Ella interjected quickly, obviously not wanting to talk about it.

Taking her cue, Heidi turned to leave. She began to put up her hood again but then stopped. Instead, as she reached for the door back to the café floor, took a deep breath, shook out her limbs, and tipped her chin towards the sky.

She was ready to face whatever was out there for the first time in days. She was ready to face the music once and for all. And Heidi realised something else.

She would ensure that Ella's Christmas party would be the best celebration the community had ever witnessed.

CHAPTER 16

"Charlie, can you bring down my hairbrush with you? I forgot to pack it in my carry-on." Ruth was panicking about her flight to LA. After hundreds of trips, one would think she would be used to travelling by now, but she still felt the same jitters as she did on her first plane ride out of Dublin decades ago.

She still felt as though she would forget something important or neglect to do something she should have before she boarded. Travelling alone was not for Ruth.

In the past, she would be with an assistant, her agent, or one of the crew from her TV show. She loved having someone to chat with, help her put her bags in the overhead storage units, or lament about the awful airline service. But today, she was flying solo.

Scarlett would stay behind with Charlie for the first time. He seemed just as nervous as Ruth about the situation, but with creche to keep her occupied and Ita invited over for dinner, he seemed to have every base covered. Ruth had even left a list of dos and don'ts for his reference. Now, all that was left was for her to say goodbye.

As her husband stomped down the stairs, hairbrush in one hand and Scarlett in his other arm, he looked just as upset as he was when Ruth had initially explained why she wanted to look at returning to acting.

"This is my dream, Charlie. This is my *career*. I cannot pass up this opportunity. Anyway, it's just a quick reading and a meeting, and then dinner with the director and casting agent. I owe it to myself to just hear them out. Who knows, they may not even offer me the movie."

Her gaze searched his for a positive response but Charlie had made it clear that he wasn't crazy about the idea. When Ruth had given up Hollywood last time it was a conscious decision between the two of them. It wasn't made lightly or without reservations. They had spent countless hours reassuring each other that she could be happy without the cameras and the flashbulbs.

But things had moved on. This was her opportunity, her last shot. In a year or two, she would be too old, too forgotten by Hollywood standards to make a go of it if she chose to. He felt that it would be unfair of him to demand that she stay. He would not watch as she grew tired, frustrated, and resentful.

So Charlie handed Ruth her hairbrush and watched as she got into the front seat of the car.

Before she drove away, he leaned into the open window and whispered, "I love you, I love you. I love you. Have fun, and remember to call us when you get in. See you in a couple of days."

Ruth flashed a brilliant smile at him, threw her arms around his neck through the open window and kissed his gruff face.

Blowing kisses at a dozing Scarlett, she said her first goodbye since she had made the decision to move back home to Lakeview. It was heartbreakingly painful, yet there was a resounding assurance that this was the right thing to do for everyone involved.

As she drove through Main Street and headed out towards the motorway, Ruth watched as the decorated artisan homes twinkled in the early morning glow.

The snow that had been steadily falling the past few hours cast a bright halo over the treetops and on the black, tiled roofs. Several people were heading out their doors to begin their day, head off to work, or fetch the morning paper and breakfast.

At the airport, she waited as the machine printed her ticket. Economy. It was all that she could afford these days with only Charlie's income and her lack of any at all. She had not flown economy in years. It was a long flight to LA, and she prayed that she would have a good, quiet seatmate to help ease the journey. There was nothing worse than being seated next to some chatty or obnoxious passenger.

She was more than relieved when she found out that she was in a row all by herself, giving her the peace and quiet she longed for.

While she tried to doze, she still found it hard to not feel the plane give and take or worry about the landing gear. Without an assistant to talk to, she couldn't be reassured.

To distract herself from her own voice in her head, she instead reviewed the lines from the script. She marked up the white pages with character notes, phrasing suggestions, and reminders or inflections. She whispered lines and recited some of the bigger monologues by memory. She had spent the last couple of days practising with Charlie and bouncing off ideas with him. Even Scarlett became a captive audience as her mum worked on her body movements and cues.

Thinking of the family she left behind, her heart ached immensely. By now, Scarlett would have fully woken up and Charlie would be on his way to creche. He had taken afternoons off from the dealership so that he could watch their daughter full-time. And he had planned out their afternoons with activities both would enjoy. He even talked about pulling her from the creche early so that they could spend time at the aquarium nearby.

His excitement and enthusiasm for caring

for their daughter was all that Ruth needed to hear. While she tried not to count her chickens, she imagined what life would be like for the family if she did get the role.

The movie would be at least 4 months' worth of work and filming both in LA and on location. Then there would be the intermittent press tours, premiers and promo that would come a year or so later. With all that, Ruth would either have to bring Scarlett on the road while Charlie stayed behind, or he would have to become a solo dad while she worked.

Either way, no option sounded appealing which is why Ruth refused to bring up the possibility. She would cross that bridge when it came.

For now, she needed to focus on nailing this reading. While it wasn't exactly an audition, the casting agent and director wanted to test her out with a potential leading man on camera. It was a nerve-racking experience despite Ruth being a pro at this sort of thing. She counted at least forty failed screen tests in her time as a working actress, and that didn't even begin to touch the number of cold auditions she had been on beforehand.

But she was resilient and moved on from each rejection. This time, however, was different. This could potentially be her last screen test, her last meeting with a director, or her last mailed script offer.

This was her final shot to make it happen. Ruth was not about to let it just slip away this time.

She was ready.

The flight passed quickly as she worked tirelessly to memorise and ingrain the words on the page. As she waited for her hired car in LAX, she felt the warm breeze of California once again and felt completely at ease.

Something about being back where the sun always shone made her journey feel complete and right. Ruth smiled as she realised that today was going to be a great day.

CHAPTER 17

The car dropped her off at the hotel first so that she could freshen up and change into more Hollywood-appropriate attire. Instead of the fitted shirts and skinny jeans she had practically lived in since moving back to Lakeview, she shimmied into a short, flared black skirt and a lacy black top.

Picking out her most daring red lipstick, she carefully applied her makeup and slipped into a pair of four-inch patent-leather heels. For the first time in a long time, she felt glam again.

Ruth arrived at the casting agency's office with a good half hour to spare. Yet, she was greeted immediately by a caravan of never-ending industry faces she vaguely remembered or recognised, from producers to lighting experts. All seemed eager to meet her and ready to work. The atmosphere was electric and she couldn't help but feel like the star she used to be.

"Ruth, we're ready for you." The casting director peeked into the waiting area and waited as she gathered her items and her script. The room was brightly lit with a white backdrop. Two cameras, one dead centre and the other off to her left as a profile, pointed at her stool.

In the darkness sat four people. Immediately, she recognised the director, one of the producers and the casting agent. The other was concealed, but she assumed it would be the leading male she would read with.

"Ruth! How good to finally meet you in person. You're as gorgeous as ever! How is life outside of Hollywood treating you?" The director, Jeff, was unexpectedly cordial. Typically directors sat in silence and the casting agent would do all the talking. She was utterly taken aback by this dynamic shift.

"It's, it's, well it's great thanks. I'm very happy."

"Well, we are very happy to have you back," the casting agent said in a bright, cheery voice. Already, Ruth was getting a great vibe from the set. "We would like you to read the monologue on page 63. Let's start at the second line down. I will read for the mother. Are you ready?"

Ruth flipped to the page, quickly scanned the acting directions she had given herself, and smiled. She had this.

"What would make you happy Annie? Would leaving the factory make you happy? Would marrying George? What do you want? What do you want!"

Ruth took a deep breath, stared directly into the camera and began.

"I want nothing more than what we all deserve. I don't want to work at the factory making peanuts-an-hour for nothing to show. I don't want to marry George or start a family with him. He's not for me. This life isn't for me. This is your life, Mama. This is your dream and your factory. I don't belong here. Don't you see? I belong somewhere where the air doesn't fill my lungs with smoke and smog, or my prospects are a man without money or another man without ambition."

As she said the last word, she knew that she had nailed it. The silence that lingered after she finished was telling. The smile on Jeff's face was promising. The claps from the casting agent were a rare feat. She oozed confidence as she recited the next three selections from memory, nailing every cue and inflection that she had practised.

"Thank you, Ruth. That was phenomenal. We would like to test you with the male lead now. We just need an idea of how you two would work on screen now if there's still any chemistry between the two of you. Troy? Are you ready?"

A voice in the darkness broke as her leading male appeared. "Are you, Ruth?"

Ruth sat motionless, unable to speak as Troy, her ex-co-star and Scarlett's birth father, sat down beside her.

CHAPTER 18

Charlie and Scarlett spent their day in a state of bliss.

With this being the first time getting his daughter all to himself, he couldn't bear to leave her at creche. Instead, the two had spent their day messing around the snow at the park by the lake, and at home playing doctor with her large collection of stuffed animals.

As she finally laid down for a nap after an action-filled day, Charlie began to prepare dinner. He knew this was an important night for his family. His mother had yet to spend more than a second inside this house since Ruth moved in. Ita refused to acknowledge

Scarlett and she had rarely called Charlie on the house number. Instead, she only interacted with him via cell phone, or when he was either at work or making a trip to see her personally.

Her blatant attempt at freezing his family out had irritated him but he understood, to an extent, the issue Ita had with their situation. For some reason she had always disliked Ruth. As a teenager, she actively tried to persuade him to not get involved with her, even when they were just studying. She instead would attempt to set him up with one of the gaggle of her friend's daughters. Each failed to catch his interest and served to infuriate and frustrate his mother more.

Ita's rage grew when she heard of their rekindled relationship, her pregnancy by another man and Charlie's acceptance of it. When she received the call from him about their engagement, she hung up without a word, too upset to say anything kind. Charlie had genuinely been hurt but knew that it would take time and love. He would prove to his mother that Ruth was the only woman for him and that Scarlett was his daughter in all but blood.

Tonight would be the night that it all came together, at least he hoped so. It had taken some persuading to get her to come, but with Ruth out of the picture for the next two days, Ita couldn't deny any pleas for her company.

The doorbell rang at exactly 6 pm. She was always on time, a trait that she had passed down to Charlie.

"Mum! Welcome! Come in, come in." He assisted her in taking off her coat and hung it in the hallway. Without a word, she surveyed their home. While not the largest, it was modest, modern and tastefully decorated with artwork Ruth had moved from her old place in LA. Every bit of the house had Ruth's touch and character. Charlie loved it.

"Scarlett, come say hello to your grandmother." The little girl walked uneasily towards Charlie, gripping his pant leg and hiding behind his arms. She was always cautious around strangers and Ita was certainly an unfamiliar face.

For her part, Ita just looked down at Scarlett and mumbled a brief greeting. She then walked off into the dining room where she sat waiting for Charlie to follow.

"How have you been, mum? I haven't heard from you in a while." He smiled at her from the other end of the table. Scarlett sat in his lap, playing with a plastic zoo animal.

"I have been doing well. I repainted your old bedroom and purchased a new sofa bed for it. I decided there wasn't much use in keeping it as a bedroom."

"No, of course not. Where did you ge—"

"Where is Miss Ruth exactly?" she interrupted him, obviously wanting to get right to the point.

"She flew back to LA on an errand," he explained patiently, sensing a trap. "She'll be back in a couple of days."

"LA?" Ita said disdainfully. "Really? And what errand is so important that she could just leave her child in the care of someone who isn't a parent?"

"Mum," he said, his voice rising, "I *am* Scarlett's parent. I adopted her. My name is on her paperwork. I *am* her father."

"Don't be stupid, Charlie," Ita countered. "You know what I mean."

"I don't think I do, Mum," he said through gritted teeth. "What exactly are you saying?"

Ita pounced. "That child is not yours," she said haughtily. "She is not your flesh and blood; she's someone else's—probably someone as irresponsible and flighty as Ruth. But where's he? Where's *she*? You're here taking care of Scarlett while her mother gallivants around Hollywood and her *real* father is God knows where. *She is not your child.*" A sense of satisfaction washed over Ita as she let that out.

"Who said she was there for work?"

"She's *obviously* up to something—a film or a TV show or something. Either way, it cannot lead to anything good but Ruth getting everything that she wants."

"And what exactly do you think Ruth wants?"

Ita smiled disdainfully. "To dump her daughter on some unsuspecting, moony-eyed idiot like you. She knows you mean money and security and she just wants to latch on like she always has. Don't you see Charlie? You are her ticket out of here and back into the limelight."

Charlie stared at his mother, utterly disgusted by the woman sitting in front of him. He put down Scarlett and allowed her to walk away to the living room where a children's cartoon played softly. "You don't know her, mum," he said, quietly seething, "and you obviously do not know me."

"Oh I know Madam Ruth well enough," she replied. "And I know her kind. She's always been selfish and self-involved, and she will only bring pain to our lives."

"*My* life, Mother," he said, his voice beginning to rise again. "There is no 'our lives,' not where Scarlett is concerned. You don't get to manage me anymore. What happens between Ruth, Scarlett and me is none of your business."

"Where my son is involved, it's *always* my business."

He stared at her icily and shook his head. "Not anymore," he reiterated, stabbing a finger in her direction. "I am tired of you talking badly about Ruth when you haven't even given her a chance. And for you to say that about Scarlett—that's my *daughter*—your *grand*daughter. I—" He slowed down, his voice shaking. "No. I'm finished. You need to leave."

"Charlie—" she said, her voice far softer now. "Now."

"You're not serious," she said as he got up

from the table and headed for the door. He opened it, ushering her out. Ita got up and looked him over one more time. "I have no idea what to say to you anymore."

"I think enough has been said already," he said coldly, his eyes locked on his mother's wrinkled, painted face.

"Will I be seeing you at Christmas?"

"Will you be welcoming my entire family or just me?" he shot back. "If the answer is just me, then I think you know the answer."

"Oh, hello!" A sweet, unexpected voice broke through the anger radiating off mother and son. Both Ita and Charlie turned to face the uninvited guest standing at the door. "I was just about to ring the bell. It looks like I have perfect timing!"

A smiling Heidi Clancy stood at the doorway, handbag in one hand and a clipboard in the other.

"What are you doing here?" Ita was on the attack. Her voice was ready to rip into her next victim.

"Well, I was hoping to talk to Charlie and Ruth, but I can kill two birds with one stone.

Do you mind if I come in? It's starting to snow again."

"No, you may not." Ita had completely taken over.

"*Excuse* me, mother," Charlie said testily. "Heidi, please come in. My mother was just leaving." Ita glanced at Charlie, and then back at his visitor. With an audible huff, she walked out of the door, narrowly missing bumping into Heidi's shoulder.

Heidi smiled awkwardly at the dishevelled man in front of her as they stood in the doorway. Both had known each other for years.

"I suppose I should explain why I am bothering you at dinner," she sighed. "I'm sure you know that Ella, the owner of café is retiring—but that's not exactly the whole story …."

Charlie had heard the rumours that the cafe was closing down but had not heard the part about Ella being forcefully evicted until earlier that day when out and about around town. The news rattled him. Ella had always been so kind and supportive to everyone in this village. But in addition to hearing about her retirement, the rumour mill was on high about Heidi's husband and their financial situation.

"OK, but I don't understand…"

"Charlie, you and I both know that Ella isn't retiring, at least not of her own volition. And I think I might have found a way to ensure that she doesn't have to. But I need some help. Do you mind if I come in?"

CHAPTER 19

*H*alf an hour later, Heidi turned to leave with a considerable spring in her step.

After spending a solid day going door to door and facing rejection after rejection, Charlie guessed that having someone like him on the case would certainly help ease her burden.

He was intrigued by her idea but wasn't sure if it had legs. Well, he'd ask around certainly. Anything to help save poor Ella from a sorry fate.

Heidi grabbed several elaborately decorated Christmas cards from her clipboard. "Here, I am having everyone who contributes sign a card for her. I already have a growing list of contributors, so if you could take another .... If you need more, just call me."

"Sure. I can't promise anything but ..."

"You have no idea how much this means for the town, Charlie. I hope we can do this. Ella deserves it. Anyway, I'll be out of your way. Say hello to Ruth for me and I look forward to hearing her perform next week."

Charlie closed the door behind her. Scarlett had been blissfully unaware of everything that had transpired as she entertained herself with her zoo animal collection and cartoons.

Once she had been fed and the dinner dishes cleared and cleaned, Charlie began to notice just how quiet the house was. Ruth had always been the life of the place.

Dinners with her were full of songs and finger puppets. She often chased Scarlett around the house pretending to be the friendly tickle monster. The shrieks of joy between the two were what kept him going every day. But in Ruth's absence, Charlie tried to remember just how life was before he became a dad and a husband.

He retrieved his phone from his coat

pocket. No calls from Ruth. She would have arrived hours ago, but he figured she was either too nervous or distracted to remember to call.

Two hours later, the phone remained silent. Scarlett had been put to bed long ago, and the house was both dark and silent.

Charlie sat up reading a book from Ruth's collection, occasionally glancing down at the device to be sure he hadn't missed her. It was just as silent.

Swallowing his pride, he made the first call. And then a second one an hour later. Then a text: "Are you all right?" It remained marked unread and unanswered.

He reassured himself that he shouldn't worry. She was fine. He knew it. She was simply at her meeting and had her phone off. Maybe she even forgot it and left it at the hotel. She was constantly forgetting her phone. This probably wasn't an exception.

But in the depths of the night with the hours ticking by, all Charlie could do was think about what his mother had suggested. Perhaps this life wasn't for Ruth after all.

Maybe she was made for important meetings with directors and agents and not for the provincial life he could give her.

Was this really the end of his wife's high-flying life, or just the beginning?

CHAPTER 20

The cold nipped at Heidi's face as she exited her car.

She grabbed her clipboard, envelope and Christmas cards as she hurried to the door. This was her third attempt at this house, but she wasn't about to take no for an answer.

She rang once. No answer. She rang again. Nothing. Lights were on inside, so she did what she had done at two others: she used the internet and her growing number of community friends to find the landline number. She could hear the phone ring from inside and then someone quickly walk or run to grab it.

"Hello!" she began in her cheeriest, most ingratiating voice, "This is Heidi. Since I know you are in, I would really appreciate it if you could open your door to me. Thank you!" She hung up and waited.

An older woman peered out as the door cracked a mere inch, enough for the woman to stick her head through. "For the third time," she scowled disdainfully, "we are not interested."

The woman's obstinance only enraged Heidi further.

"Mrs McGrath," she pressed, "I understand that you said no the last time. But since we last spoke, I have learned from some very reliable sources that you frequent the café for breakfast on a regular basis. You cannot make me believe that when Ella closes up shop for good, that you won't miss her or her wonderful Irish fry-ups." Eric McGrath's mother squinted her beady eyes at Heidi, clearly both impressed and irritated at her salesmanship. "I'm not asking for much. I just ask that you give what you can. It could be ten euros, twenty—whatever you can contribute. Your money will go directly to paying off the outstanding liabilities. Nobody but the bank will touch a cent of it."

Heidi then smiled at the woman who had

only allowed her head to show. Without a word, Maeve turned, leaving the door partially open. Heidi didn't dare to take a step inside. Moments passed, but when she returned she handed her a cheque that was far more generous than she'd expected. Without a word, Heidi handed her the Christmas card to sign and left with a loud thank you.

Back in her car, she took out her notepad. With the McGrath's donation, and with the help and time of Charlie, she had raised quite a lot of money already.

Based on the outstanding liabilities though, it would take a lot more than that to bring the arrears back into credit and make the bank lift the repossession order.

That number sank in. With only a week left until the party, the full amount seemed impossible. Heidi had hit up every single house in the village and had even ventured to nearby communities for help. Her persistence had paid off. Just like Maeve McGrath, most households gave in to Heidi's requests on the second or third try.

She used tactics like spying on frequent customers and having her mother Betty and sister-in-law Kim track down others for the cause, and Conor Dempsey, a popular local businessman (and another part of Heidi's family of sorts), tap up some of his corporate golf buddy clients.

Her network had pulled off a miracle, yet they were still far short of what was needed.

Still, Heidi couldn't help but feel satisfied. For the first time in her life, she had accomplished something on her own. And even more so, the community had actually turned itself around on her. While she was not looking to change her own reputation, she could feel that she was respected and taken more seriously than she was when word of Paul's job loss hit.

Her only problem was just that—Paul had little idea what she was up to when she left for the day. Heidi had promised she was out job searching, but she hadn't even attempted to find work. She was too busy focusing on this one task.

Next, she pulled out a map of the village. Little marks denoted homes, businesses and the names of the owners. She had made a big "X" through the mark when a family had donated. And she highlighted those she had yet to go to or who had refused her. She was glad to cross the McGrath house off the list. It would be the last of this row to hold out on a donation. Even that itself was a major accomplishment that could not be ignored.

But there was no time to waste. With so few days left, Heidi had to practically double her outreach. Using her index finger, she searched and scanned the map for any other Lakeview homes or businesses that she may have missed.

In the western corner, a little way outside town she found the riding stables. Of course! The place was brimming with regulars to the café and the owner, Joseph Evans, was forever holding up the counter in there. In her eagerness to grab all donors from the town itself, she had completely forgotten about this potential goldmine.

Heidi sped out of the town centre and headed up the hill towards the stables situated in a woodland area outside Lakeview.

As she entered a small reception just in front of the old stone building, a young woman greeted her with a reserved smile. "How can I help you?"

"I am looking for Mr Evans," she explained,

batting her eyes serenely in an attempt to look both innocent and appealing. "Would he happen to be in?"

"He is, but I am afraid Joseph is busy at the moment. Can I ask what this is in reference to?"

"I'm here about the café. I am a friend of the owner, Ella and am in the process of—"

A tall, grey-haired man suddenly appeared in a doorway nearby. He looked at Heidi with concern.

"I'm sorry Nina, I thought I heard something about the café. I can take over from here." He gestured for Heidi to join him in his small office. Quickly, he gathered up the maps and papers that littered the chairs and desk.

She sat in the first empty one she could find.

"Mr. Evans, it is great to meet you. I am Heidi Clancy, and as I said, I am here about the Heartbreak Café. As you may have heard Ella, the owner is planning on closing the restaurant after Christmas. While she is saying that she is retiring, the real reason is that her building is being repossessed. But I believe that the Heartbreak Café can and must be saved. It is a vital part of our community and culture and I am sure that your customers and staff—all frequent café patrons—can and will agree. At this time, I have raised a substantial amount of money to clear the arrears and stave off the repossession order, but it is not yet enough. And that is why I am here."

Heidi paused, waiting for the man to say something. Instead, he just stared at her with his hands cupped in front of his mouth, concealing his emotions.

"I understand that times are hard and that you may not be able to give much, but if you are able to contribute even a little I'd be grateful for any donation to be used to pay off the outstanding arrears."

Again, Heidi waited but the man just looked directly at her.

"So would you be willing to contribute something to help save the café?" She had exhausted her entire sales pitch. Yet this man just sat there like a stone gargoyle passing judgment.

"What was your name again?"

"Heidi Clancy.

"Can I ask you a question, Ms Clancy? Do

you happen to know the owner of the building—the person who is directly responsible for evicting Ella from the café she has run for almost thirty years?"

Heidi sank into her chair. She had imagined this happening several times, yet no one had yet to ask her about her conflict of interest. And now, she was found out. While she had every intention of saving the café and none at all for improving her family's financial situation, she knew how this had to look to someone in the know.

"Yes, I do. And Paul Clarke is indeed my husband, but please allow me to explain…"

"I am not sure there is much explaining to do. Despite Ella's dutiful payment of rent, your husband is underwater on the property. And here you are, trying to get the community to chip in and pay your debts? While I have never seen this kind of scheme before, I have to admit it's a good one. You almost had me believe that this *was* charity." Joseph's eyes burned bright in anger. He leaned forward, practically hovering over his desk.

"I know how this appears. I do. But please believe me when I say that this has nothing to do with my family situation. My husband lost his job at the bank ... he'd got behind on the repayments of some of his portfolio ... I had no idea how awful the situation was, or that other people would be affected. Please believe me. I am here because Ella is my friend and she deserves to keep the café. She has been good to me. She has defended me when no other would even glance at me. She's been a rock; a loyal ally to so many of us, and I cannot imagine this town without her or the café. This is why I'm here if you want to know the truth. I'm here to make this right."

Heidi's voice was firm, yet sincere. While she knew there was little chance of him believing her, she had to try to explain her side of the story. At this point, she didn't care what he thought about her personally.

"Does Ella know you're doing this?"

"No. At least, I don't think so. Every donor I have found so far has been told not to say anything because I don't know if we'll have enough..."

"And how much exactly, have you raised?"

She momentarily let her guard down and let her pride shine through. "Approximately a quarter of the outstanding arrears in little under a week."

Joseph nodded, clearly impressed by her accomplishment. "And how much more is needed to stave off the repossession order?"

Heidi held her breath as she whispered the number to him.

"Does your husband know that you're involved in this?"

"No. This is my cause, not his."

After a very long pause, Joseph spoke. "I'm sorry, I think I understand why you are doing it and I admire that. But I very much doubt that you can achieve what you need to in such a short space of time."

Heidi sighed. She supposed that deep down she'd realised that all along. But she'd still felt she needed to do *something*. Be it out of pride, guilt or god forbid the goodness of her heart.

"However as I said, I admire your ambition and clearly you are a determined lady." Then Joseph paused, his eyes twinkling. "But now I wonder if you could utilise some of that same determination to do something for me…"

CHAPTER 21

"Paul? Can you bring down all the boxes labelled 'Christmas Indoor Lighting?'" Heidi shouted loudly at her husband who was currently rummaging around in their attic. "Oh. And grab that blue bucket of baubles underneath the box of summer clothes."

She impatiently watched as her husband brought box after box down from the attic. Each one was full to the brim with holiday decorations they had planned to donate or leave behind now that the move from their beloved house was all but finalised.

Exhausted, Paul looked at her as if she was

crazy and then when she'd finally finished her list of requests, retreated to his study.

She couldn't blame him for not understanding why she was still so heavily involved in the café Christmas party. After all, their entire lives were now in boxes and her going through some of the most useless ones seemed pointless considering the comings and goings of their life.

They'd decided to sell the house to Paul's interested friend and use any profit from the sale to pay off some of the outstanding debt, which was also where much of her husband's redundancy package was going.

The sale was going through at the moment, and after Christmas, the family were moving in with Heidi's parents until they found something else, perhaps something smaller to rent.

Betty and Mick had been insistent, although Heidi had nearly died of shame having to admit to her folks and the entire Clancy family the full extent of her and Paul's situation.

But to be fair, her siblings and in-laws were wonderful, Kim even going as far as to offer Heidi a job in her beauty products company.

"Clearly you're a born saleswoman," her sister-in-law had joked, referring to Heidi's efforts thus far at raising money for the café, "and I could really do with another rep."

Though it still broke Heidi's heart to see her beloved home sold out from beneath her, she knew that there were worse things.

So in the New Year, the family would be completely moved out and Heidi would be going to work for the first time in her thirty-odd year life.

But seeing the brown boxes all taped up with labels like 'sell ASAP' or 'from Amelia's nursery' depressed her to the core. While she had begun to accept a lifestyle that wasn't all glitz and glamour, going cold turkey with her savings had been traumatic enough. Yet she knew she would get over it in time, with the help of family, friends and a new purpose.

But with the café Christmas party less than twenty-four hours away, Heidi couldn't help but feel a bit out of sorts. She truly had no idea how her family would survive all these changes. She had hoped that Paul would quickly find a job in his old industry, but he'd had no luck securing interviews or even meetings with former colleagues.

Instead, he had spent hours upon hours in his office working on business plans for his remaining investments. While she was doing her utmost to put Ella's building back in the black, he was content working on something of his own.

He seemed to actually enjoy the hands-on aspect of managing the properties instead of from afar, which was what had got him into trouble in the first place. At dinner several nights ago, he'd even casually mentioned something about perhaps trying to do something in rental property maintenance. While he managed to keep his optimism at bay, Heidi could feel hope coming back to him.

It seemed that both Heidi and Paul had new roles to fill now, but while he had kept her up to date on his plans, she neglected to fill him in on her stint as a small business activist and town fundraising mogul.

She wasn't sure how he would take it. Her attempt to save the café was ultimately at his expense, and she didn't know how he would feel if she knew she'd been basically asking the entire community for a handout to pay back his financial misadventures.

It would be a blow to any man's ego.

Early on, she had made a plan to keep her actions a secret. Firstly, she had all correspondence from the bank regarding the building forwarded to her and she had been keeping the local estate agent up to date on her efforts so he wouldn't unexpectedly sell the property without her knowledge.

All this and still she wasn't sure that it would be enough. Especially given Joseph Evan's request last week.

Yet she had come so far, and she was not about to give up just yet. With one day until the party, she just needed to hold Paul off for twenty-four more hours by keeping him out of town (where someone might mention Heidi's door-to-door soliciting) and more importantly away from the party preparations.

The truth was she didn't know if Paul would go to the party at all. She knew he wasn't much in the mood for celebrating and she guessed that the last thing he wanted was to face the community in the wake of his disgrace.

Once Heidi had finished loading the car, she began to make her retreat. "Okay, I got what I needed," she called back to her husband, "and I'm taking Amelia to the café with me. We'll be back around eight. Do you need me to grab anything while I'm in town?"

Paul peeked his head out of the office as she zipped up Amelia's coat. "Actually, I was thinking about going down with you. I'd like to talk to Ella ... maybe try to explain. And I'm sure you will need help with decorating the place."

"No, no we're totally fine! Ella's son is there and Colm too - that's more than enough people to help with the decorating." She tried her best not to snipe at him or to look him directly in the eyes. "Anyway, this is Ella's big night so I'm not sure now is the best time. It might only drag her down."

"Oh, OK. You're right of course. For what it's worth, tell her I'm sorry anyway, OK?"

"Sure. I'll give you a full report when I get back." Heidi kissed Paul, scooped up Amelia and headed out the garage door. She briefly turned to smile and wave after settling her daughter in her car seat.

Paul still watched somewhat dazedly from the doorway and she felt sorry for him having to hide away from everyone.

Heidi gulped, realising that tomorrow night she was about to do the very opposite. The whole village would be at the party and some of them would be whispering, pointing and looking down their noses at her.

Yet, she realised taking heart, as she drove over the stone bridge and towards the café, snow gently falling around them, that there would be many others, including Ella who would empathise with her family's woes and go out of their way to include in the celebrations.

She was one of Lakeview's own after all.

CHAPTER 22

*E*lla waited for Heidi in her now-completely empty café.

In all her life, she had never seen the place without the signature picture frames on the wall, the old Singer table in the corner or the cherry red bar stools at the counter. Colm and the staff had done much of the work for her, allowing her to supervise from a chair in the corner.

After the furniture was gone, the few folding tables and chairs Heidi had borrowed from the community hall arrived, just as Joseph walked through the door.

As he had promised, he still visited Ella at the café every single day. Today would be no exception as he helped her son, Dan and the remaining staff unfold and unbox the supplies and even supervised the laying out of the empty trays to be filled tomorrow.

The place buzzed with both anticipation and sadness. Tomorrow would be the last time her staff gathered here, and Ella was not about to waste it. She had already begun to hand out cards with heartfelt thanks and letters of recommendation to those she knew would want to move on quickly. There were hugs and memories shared while old and new joked and sang festive tunes to help keep spirits up.

Whenever she felt herself get emotional, Ella reminded herself that this party was exactly how her father-in-law and husband would have wanted their cafe days to end.

This ode to her loved ones was not only her way of getting closure but also a way to honour the community that made the café what it was —a Lakeview institution. Therefore, everything would be perfect—from the mulled wine to the last mince pie. She wouldn't take anything less.

Just as Ella began to supervise the kitchen

cleanup crew, Heidi walked in holding Amelia's hand and a large blue bucket in her other hand.

"Perfect weather for a Christmas party, isn't it?" Her cheeks were bright pink from the chill in the air, but her eyes were lit up with energy. It was a complete change from the run-down, beat-up Heidi that came into her café barely two weeks prior.

"Let me help you with that Heidi," Joseph grabbed the heavy container from her arms and set it down in the corner.

"I didn't know you two knew each other?" Ella couldn't imagine where Heidi could have met Joseph.

"Oh, I know Joseph from ….when one time Paul and I were thinking about getting Amelia a pony. He gave us great advice." She was totally floundering but she couldn't give away anything. Either way, it didn't seem as if Ella was paying too much attention. Her gaze was set on Amelia in her cute festive outfit.

"Would you like to help me taste some Christmas cookies pet? I think there are some Santa ones with your name on them." Amelia giggled excitedly as she rushed to Ella's side. They disappeared in the back, leaving Joseph and Heidi alone to sort through the decorations and supplies.

As the two leaned down to untangle the lighting, Joseph whispered, "Are we all set for tomorrow?"

"Yep. Just be ready at eight sharp. Santa is supposed to arrive at that time, which I think would be just the right moment."

CHAPTER 23

By the time the group had finished, the café was completely illuminated by large, white bulbs that arched from the wooden ceilings.

Garlands of silver red and gold intertwined along the wall lamps, and a medium-sized picture-postcard fir tree adorned with Heidi's finest designer decorations sat in the far corner where a keyboard, microphone and Santa's chair would be set up.

As the last twinkling bauble was hung with care, Ella reappeared with Amelia in hand.

"So pwetty!" The little girl ran to the centre of the room, excitedly jumping and spinning under the sparkling lights and the shadow of the tree.

Ella was similarly entranced. "Oh it looks beautiful Heidi, you've done an amazing job." She took the younger woman's hand. "Thank you, I mean that. I know you and Paul will both go on to better things."

"No, thank *you*." Heidi was overcome with emotion and gratitude for this lovely lady who by rights should hate her guts. "Come on, Amelia," she sniffed. "We better get going if we want to get a good night's sleep. I have a feeling that a very special visitor might be here tomorrow and we want to get our beauty rest for it." She turned again to face Ella and Joseph. "See you tomorrow at around four, OK? Ruth and Nicky will be in at five to set up the music. And the party will officially begin at six. I think that gives us just enough time to get everything ready. But if you need anything else, just let me know."

She quickly grabbed her empty containers and Amelia's coat before taking off, leaving only Joseph and Ella in the café.

It was now silent, save for the Dean Martin

festive classics playing softly in the background.

For a long moment, the two stared at each other, unsure of what to say.

Joseph went first. "Yes, the place indeed looks beautiful. It reminds me of how it all used to be." He looked around the café noting just how so much and so little had managed to change since he first moved to the village.

"It does," Ella said, blushing. She couldn't seem to feel anything but uncomfortable in his presence now, especially given her recent realisation. "It really does." She sighed and turned towards him. "Listen," she began apologetically, "I wanted to talk to you. I've been meaning to apologise for the way I acted the day I told you about the eviction."

Joseph shook his head. "Let's not talk about this tonight," he reassured her. "Let's focus on what is happening here and now."

"What's happening here and now?" Ella looked up into his eyes that now practically danced beneath the twinkling lights.

"Us." Joseph leaned down, gently kissed her forehead, and then slowly walked towards the door. She remained motionless, too stunned to speak. "See you tomorrow, Ella."

She stood alone in the centre of the room for a very long time after that. It was as if her whole life had flashed back and then forward with one innocent kiss. And reminded her of what she had and what she was about to lose.

Yet now in the silence of the empty café, Ella couldn't help but wonder if this was what she'd actually wanted all along.

CHAPTER 24

"Charlie? *Charlie!* Are you ready? We are *so late*. Ella is going to kill me."

Ruth darted down the stairs while pinning her hair into a tight bun. She grabbed her black velvet Louboutin heels and quickly tossed them on.

"Charlie!" she yelled again. "Let's go!" She hated to be late, and at ten minutes to five, she feared that she would have no time to warm up her vocal cords or to practice with the keyboard player.

"Go on ahead without us if you like," Charlie replied. "We'll take the van." His voice wasn't in the least bit rushed; in fact, it was perfectly monotone. His lack of urgency irritated Ruth—not because he refused to be ready in time, but because he had been acting like this since she got back from LA.

She could still feel his coldness as she'd walked through the door from the airport, bags still in hand.

Scarlett had run to greet her with a hug and to ask if she had brought anything back for her, but Charlie remained in the kitchen pretending to be preoccupied with dinner. When she found him, he walked up to her, rubbed her shoulders and kissed her cheek—hardly the effusive welcome she had pictured.

The next few days were more of the same. Charlie had thrown himself into his work by volunteering to pick up an entire week's worth of daytime sales shifts and be the night-time mechanic on-call. When Ruth did see him, he practically ignored her and instead focused on Scarlett or another part of the house like the broken step or the frosty path out front.

Ruth had so much to tell him about her trip, the reading, and her meeting, yet he never gave her the chance to talk about it. When she announced that she had been offered the part, he interrupted her, changed the subject completely and then excused himself to prepare for work. She never got to explain herself or the situation.

And with the way their relationship was going, she was afraid that whatever was going on in Charlie's mind would eventually boil over.

She just hoped it wouldn't be tonight.

Tonight she would be returning to her roots. She wasn't just going to be Charlie Mellon's wife or the girl that used to be in that TV show. No, this time, Ruth was stepping out as someone entirely different.

Before heading out the door, she checked herself in the mirror one last time. Her red satin dress looked fabulous on her lightly tanned skin. She smiled at herself while repeating *"This is going to be a great night!"* over and over again in her head. She just wished she believed her own mantra.

Ruth sped towards the café, eager to try to arrive at least within ten minutes of when she said she would. She parked the car, and straightening her low-cut figure-hugging dress quickly ran inside.

Once through the door, she gasped. The

café that she had known and loved all these years had been magically transformed by the dimmed lights and the glittering decor. A tree straight out of a magazine spread stood at the back and a musician dressed in a suit and tie, Colm's partner Nicky waited next to it, checking his watch.

"What. Are. You. Doing. Here." The direct, pointed question suddenly cut through Ruth like a knife. She spun on her heel to face the voice.

"Ita, hello. How are you doing?" Ruth plastered on a fake smile, wide enough that her teeth showed like an animal ready for a fight. "What am I doing here?" she continued. "I am Ella's friend and a loyal member of this community. I have every right to be here."

"Pah!" The contempt in her mother-in-law's voice was unsettling and Ruth could tell by the way Ita sauntered slowly and feebly over to her that she had already been drinking the mulled wine.

"Plus, she asked me to perform at the party, so I am here and happy to help."

"And how much did you demand to be paid?"

"Excuse me?" Ruth wasn't completely sure where Ita was going with that.

"Don't play stupid with me, madam. I know that the likes of you would do just about anything for money." Ita's voice echoed around the nearly empty room, and Ruth spotted some of the volunteer staff's gaze moving to the two, watching and waiting for what would happen next.

"I'm sorry, but I need to speak with Nicky now so we can warm up and be ready for when the party begins." It was all Ruth could do to compose herself. She walked away from Ita, leaving her standing alone in the centre of the room clutching her glass of mulled wine.

By the way, she was smiling, Ruth could tell that Ita felt like she had won something. What, she wasn't sure.

She distracted herself with her music partner's notes. Nicky handed her a stack of sheet music and played a bit of every song to give her an idea of what key would begin each one. He then assisted her by playing a couple of vocal warmups. Ruth was ready, but she had yet to spot Ella for further direction.

While Nicky went outside to take a call,

Ruth ran to the back in hopes of finding the hostess there. Unsuccessful, she found a volunteer placing cookies on the trays. He pointed her to the closed office door in the far corner.

Ruth knocked and let herself in. Inside, Ella sat in tears, her head in her hands, Heidi kneeling alongside her.

"Gosh, I'm so sorry," Ruth blushed, mortified. "I should have waited for you to tell me to come in." She looked over at Heidi, who had already exhausted a box of tissues.

"Nonsense," Ella insisted, collecting herself. "Come on in. I'm just a little emotional today. I thought I would be ready to say goodbye but here I am, blubbering like a baby."

Ruth took a seat next to the older woman and reached over to pat her on the back of her deep jade velvet dress. "It's all right," she said consolingly, "I completely understand. I mean, you're losing a part of you that you never thought you could give up. That's tough."

"She's right," Heidi said, wiping her own eyes. "This place has been yours for so many years, and..." She trailed off and shook her head, composing herself. "But today is a new day Ella. It's not an end; it's a beginning."

Ruth thought this was a little bit rich coming from Heidi Clancy, considering. She'd heard about her fundraising exploits and wasn't entirely sure how to feel about them. Yet she seemed genuinely concerned for Ella now.

"You're both right," Ella smiled. "I just thought I had come to terms with it by now. I don't know. I suppose it's silly but I've never been one to give up on a desperate case. My cats and dogs will tell you that."

Ruth smiled and handed her a fresh tissue from her clutch bag. She patted her shoulder reassuringly.

"No one would ever think that you're silly," she said.

"Yes, you mean everything to this town. *Every*thing. You'll see tonight." Heidi winked at Ruth, who had no idea what to decipher from that. Had her fundraising come good after all? She couldn't see how...

"Come on. It's almost six, and I already saw a line outside waiting for you to open the doors," Heidi urged Ella. "Let's go out there and throw the best damn Christmas party this place has ever seen."

Ella nodded, smiled, and dabbed her eyes. She used a small pocket mirror to check the rest of her makeup and then boldly opened the door.

"Colm," she said, "are we ready?"

"We are sweetheart," he confirmed, smiling. "Are you?"

Ella dabbed her eyes one more time and straightened her dress. "Yes," she replied, smiling through her tears.

It was time to say goodbye.

CHAPTER 25

A few volunteers gathered at the front of the café as people began to stream in, each batting light snowfall off of their shoes and coats before entering.

Ella welcomed them all with a warm hug while Heidi passed out mince pies and glasses of mulled wine. The guests then dispersed around the room, each stopping to look at the old photos from down through the years that Ella had put on display.

Love and friendship filled the small space within minutes. It was beyond Ella's wildest expectations. Every corner was packed with customers—friends. Everyone had kind words to say about the café—a moment or a memory they wanted to reminisce about.

When Paul tentatively arrived with Amelia a few minutes later, he spotted Heidi and waved at her from across the crowded room. She smiled back, proud that her husband had in the end decided to show his face, but her face quickly fell as she spotted the Lakeview Mum's Club following closely behind.

Cynthia was in the lead (of course) and her husband towing ten steps behind as if being dragged on a leash. Deirdre and Emer quickly followed, obviously perturbed at the lack of space in the tight room. Paul's sister Gemma and her husband entered last, clearly looking out of place and unwilling to join in.

Heidi held her breath as she made her way to the entrance. She gave Amelia a hug and kissed Paul. She then faced the women.

"Hello ladies," she said in the kindest tone she could muster. "Welcome to the party. Here are your tickets for the kids' carriage ride. They have a time on them but if you need to exchange for an earlier time, feel free to swap with someone."

To the surprise of no one—least of all Heidi—Cynthia took the opportunity to be catty.

"I never took you for a horsey kind, Heidi," she crowed sarcastically, "but then again, I never believed you when you said you were hosting this party in the first place. Tell me, is Ella paying you for this or are you just hoping to network for a job as a stable girl?"

The three laughed at Cynthia's 'wit' while their husbands slipped away.

Heidi ignored them. Impressing or entertaining these women was no longer on her agenda. Instead, she whispered hello to Gemma and offered to hang her coat.

"I heard you were doing some *fundraising*," Cynthia called at her as she walked away and Paul put down his drink and looked interested. "You stopped at every house but mine. I wonder why that is? Is it because you knew I wouldn't help or was it because you knew that *I* knew exactly what you were up to?" Cynthia had been waiting for this moment, Heidi could feel it. Every word she said was calculated and uttered at a rate that was slow and deliberate.

"I'm sorry, what's all this?" Paul asked, looking searchingly at Heidi.

"That's right," Gemma sneered. "I know that while you have been pretending to raise money for Ella, all along you have been raising the money for your husband. If you were able to save this place, your husband's debt on it would be paid, or is there another scheme you are working on? Con artists like you always seem to have something up their sleeves."

Half of the party had now turned to watch. Christmas carols playing softly over the loudspeaker were practically the only other sound. Heidi scanned the room for Ella, but she was nowhere to be seen. She was most likely in the back, preparing to refill the drinks bowl or gathering up more food.

"Heidi, what is going on?" Paul looked at her sternly.

She tried to explain. "Honey, I was just helping Ella. I owed it to her, so I helped her out by raising money to try and pay back the arrears."

"Raising money from this community to pay our debts? Why? Why would you do that? You know what this looks like, surely?" His anger was growing, as faces burned a hole into the couple.

Taking a deep breath, Heidi took her husband's hand and turned and faced the onlookers.

"I didn't try to do this for Paul or myself," she told the crowd. "I tried because Ella is the one person in this village that deserves our love and respect. She doesn't deserve to be evicted. I know what Paul did was wrong." She faced her husband directly. "But he didn't mean …*we* never meant for this to happen." Her voice was passionate, pleading. "I never meant to swindle or deceive anyone either. I just wanted what was best for Ella."

"I believe you, Heidi." Ruth's voice reached over the tops of everyone's head.

"I believe you too," Colm chorused and Ella's staff also followed, joining Ruth as they made their way to Heidi.

"A true Clancy woman never goes down without a fight." Kim, Heidi's sister-in-law, suddenly appeared from nowhere and stood beside her, along with her brother Ben and the rest of the Clancy family.

"I believe you too," Her other sister-in-law piped in quietly. Cynthia and the girls shot

Paul's sister Gemma a look that permanently sealed her fate in that group.

Then, much to Heidi's amazement, similar agreeable mumbles began to pop up around the café, as Lakeview friends and neighbours gathered around Heidi to shield her from the dreaded Mummy Martyrs.

And for once, Heidi's delighted heart swelled with well-earned pride.

S**POTTING SOMEONE OUTSIDE**, Ruth ran to the back of the room as she spotted Ella entering, party platter in hand. "Merry Christmas, everyone," she called out huskily over the microphone. "While we know it's not the big night just yet, I heard that a very special visitor is making his way to Lakeview a couple of days early. Let's give a big round of applause for the man himself, Santa Claus!"

On cue, in walked a very convincing Santa Claus complete with long white beard, red velvet suit and black boots.

He greeted each child as he made his way to the back of the room. Children gathered around him, all ready to unload their holiday wish lists.

Ella watched from the kitchen, smiling at her Santa Claus. But as she set down the platter, Heidi approached her in a hurry, looking panicked.

"Ella, Ella. The carriage is here, but there's some kind of problem! I think there's something wrong with one of the horses."

CHAPTER 26

*E*lla looked at Heidi quizzically. She had no idea what could be wrong with the horses and if there was, what she could do about it. Obviously, Joseph was otherwise engaged in Santa duties, but if there was an issue with one of the animals, someone would have surely told him in advance. She put down the platter and quickly grabbed her coat and a hat from the kitchen.

"Did they say what was wrong?"

"No. But it sounded bad."

"Of all things to go wrong, horses shouldn't be one of them."

As Ella made her way through the back door of the kitchen, she could hear Santa make an announcement over the speaker, yet there was no time to hear exactly what was being said.

"Ho, Ho, Ho!" he called out jovially. "Before I begin, I have a present for someone very special here tonight. While I know it's snowing and cold out there, can you all join me lakefront outside to where my carriage awaits?"

Santa led the group of partygoers outside and around the corner towards the lake, each curiously following behind in clusters of families and neighbours.

Ella was already out there trying to talk to Eric McGrath, one of Joseph's staff.

"What do you mean you can't let the kids ride in the carriages? That's exactly what they're for, didn't Joseph tell you about the plan? This is for the town, Eric!" she pleaded, but he just smiled and shook his head while Heidi stood alongside, not a peep out of her.

"Is there a problem here?" Santa tapped Ella on the shoulder and she turned in shock to see practically the entire village, now gathered outside the café by the lake; fairy lights on the nearby trees illuminating their expectant faces. She took a couple of steps back in surprise.

"Just a little snag with the carriage rides, Jos ... erm, Santa. We'll get it sorted out in no time. How about we all go back inside?" She began to walk towards the door to the kitchen, yet no one moved. Everyone just watched her, smiling.

"Ella, my dear," Joseph began with a wink, "How about you sit up in this carriage - Santa has a special present for you."

She nervously took his hand as he hoisted her up in the old-style open-top carriage's rear seat, placing her walking cane in her lap. Then stood on the step, elevated in front of the crowd.

"As you may have heard, these are our last days in the town's beloved Heartbreak Cafe, for it is closing soon. When I first heard this, I was extremely upset. It was always my favourite place to stop on my Christmas rounds. That's when Heidi suggested to help out. While my elves can build toys and wrap presents, they cannot make everything in the workshop."

He grinned and Ella chuckled nervously. Oh, so it was a going-away present, how lovely. She guessed a bunch of roses or a box of chocolates or something.

"See, Santa knows that Ella hasn't exactly been a good girl recently. She told a little white lie to make us all feel better about her departure. It seems as though she didn't really want to retire, but had to because of reasons beyond her control. So with a little bit of Christmas magic and a whole lot of help from almost everyone in Lakeview, let me present Ella with our special gift. Heidi?"

He moved out of the way as Heidi hopped into the carriage in the seat across. She quietly handed Ella an envelope and her hands shook as she opened it.

Heidi's eyes were wet. "We couldn't bear to let you leave, Ella. We love you. The whole community loves you."

As she perused the envelope's contents, Ella's breath hitched audibly. Her jaw dropped and tears began to stream down her cheeks and onto her coat.

Inside was another letter from the same estate agent as before, this time announcing that the repossession order on the building had been lifted, and she was free to continue trading.

"How? When?" Her voice was shaking.

"Everyone chipped in to help pay off the arrears. Some gave a couple of euros, some gave hundreds. But we did it, Ella. We saved the café."

How on earth? And Heidi of all people….

Now Heidi had too begun to cry and laugh all at the same time, as Ella flung herself at her for a huge, grateful hug.

CHAPTER 27

After several overwhelming minutes, Ella turned to face the crowd. "This is too much. How will I ever repay you all?"

"More muffins! Free coffee!" a voice amid the gathering cried as laughter erupted.

Ella stood up, balancing herself on Heidi's arm. She felt that she did need to say something more though. Her gratitude was overflowing.

"When I first met my husband and his family all those years ago, I was just another Lakeview girl. I loved this town. Every bit of it. From the neighbours who always had a kind word, to the way that the hair salon always knew when you were due for a trim.

But my favourite place in the world was this café. As many of you know, it was where I met my husband Gregory, where we shared our first kiss and where I last said goodbye to him the night he passed on." She looked down at her hands, choking back tears but then ploughed on. "It's the place where all of our kids took their first steps, where they learned to talk, and definitely where they picked up a sweet tooth." Grinning, she looked up and waved at her smiling eldest son Dan, near the front.

"When I was left alone to run this place, I wasn't sure I could do it. I wasn't sure I could retain the same welcoming environment that you have all grown to love. But every day, customers would still arrive. Every day, you ordered your cups of tea, your Irish breakfasts, your ham sandwiches. And even though it was still so hard to just get through another day alone, there was always someone there with a smile and a friendly hello.

One night, I swore to myself and to my family's memory that I would keep this place alive in honour of their legacy and spirit. I would make it the place they had dreamed it to be. And thanks to devoted staff members like Colm, Nina and the gang, it has been. But still, I never knew how much this place meant to me until I thought I was going to have to leave it and that my days here were numbered. Today, you have given me back my home, my family, and my heart. There is no better Christmas gift. Thank you all. Thank you so much."

The crowd clapped as whistles and hollers were cried out and Ella sat down, waving at friendly and familiar faces blowing her kisses and nodded happily.

Then Heidi stood up to speak, her voice shaking from the emotion of the moment. "Now, I think it is time for our first carriage ride around the lake! You all have your tickets for Christmas by the Lake, so be sure to meet here or miss out. Ella and Santa, will you do the honour of leading the first group?"

Joseph laughed as he promptly got in the carriage next to Ella. He pulled the blanket up to his lap and waved at the crowd as he shouted his promises to the children to be back shortly for visits.

Heidi stepped out of the carriage as Ella

grabbed her hand, "You, my dear, are something else."

Heidi smiled, more grateful for a friend than ever. She leaned over and whispered into Ella's ear. As Heidi caught her up, she looked in shock. Heidi continued giving her more and more details on the situation and when she was finished, Ella smiled brightly and turned to Santa, her hand grasping his.

"Eric," Heidi called to the driver of the carriage, "I think we're ready now!"

The horses ambled off as Heidi stayed behind. She organised the next group by having them line up in families or groups of six. As they boarded, she took their ticket and waved them off, horses making tracks in the snow. Kim was right. She was a good organiser.

The rest of the crowd eventually began to disperse back inside where Heidi could hear Ruth and the pianist begin to perform.

"I am so proud of you honey." Paul wrapped his arms around her and she spun around to face him. Her husband's face was bright for the first time in weeks.

"I am so sorry I didn't tell you. I wanted to, but I didn't know how you would react."

"It's OK. It really is."

"No, it isn't. I should have told you. I shouldn't have risked your reputation like that. You're my husband and you deserved to know and at least have a say in what I was doing. I am finished with lying. From now on, I am going to be one hundred percent honest with you, no matter what." She waited for him to begin scolding her, and agree with what she was saying.

But he shook his head. "What you did here tonight and this week was amazing. While I'm not thrilled that you lied, I am thrilled that you are who you are and that I'm the one married to you. This is a side of you I have never seen. It's like falling in love with a completely new person." He chuckled.

"Merry Christmas, honey," she whispered, inwardly swelling with pride.

"Merry Christmas to you too, sweetheart. Now let's go back inside. I'm freezing, and Amelia is being watched by Kim. We'd better save her before her aunt starts giving her mulled wine."

CHAPTER 28

Inside the café, Ruth was just getting started. She was leading the entire crowd in carols and old Christmas favourites that everyone knew or could easily catch onto. Children excitedly ran through the gathering as the adults joined arms and sang along with neighbours and loved ones. The music and jubilant atmosphere was infectious.

Ruth looked out at the crowd as she crooned into the mic. It seemed like everyone was here in this tiny space—everyone but Charlie and Scarlett. She'd hoped she had missed them, that they were perhaps hiding in the kitchen waiting for her set to finish or maybe running behind in hopes of missing the crowd.

But as time passed, the only member of her family that remained in the room was Ita.

It was hard not to spot her. Out of all the happy faces, her mother-in-law's was solemn. Dressed head to toe in mourning black, she sat at the front table glaring at Ruth. That warring exchange they'd had earlier obviously wasn't done. And as Ruth's first set neared its break, she tried to plan an exit strategy to avoid all and any contact with this woman.

As the last song played, Ruth gave her, "We'll be back shortly! Enjoy the mulled wine responsibly," joke and turned to face Nicky, pretending to converse in order to avoid speaking with anyone else. Then she grabbed her phone and sent a text message:

"Charlie! Where are you? What is going on? My first set just ended and your mother is here. Please come soon with Scarlett."

As she hit send, Ita, now sloppily drunk, approached her. *"Weshoultak,"* she said, slurring.

"Excuse me?" Ruth replied, an eyebrow raised.

Ita composed herself and tried again. "We should talk," she responded.

"I'm just gonna go grab a bottle of water, and then we can talk if I have time before I go on again."

"No," Ita shouted loudly at the back of Ruth's head as she walked away. "I want to talk to you *now*."

Ruth spun on her toes and hurried off towards the kitchen, Ita on her heels. Cornered, she had no choice but to confront her mother-in-law. "What do you want, Ita?" Ruth whispered, low but stern hoping that they wouldn't draw any more attention.

"You couldn't stay away, could you?" Ita hissed. "I knew from the moment he met you—I *knew* that you were going to be trouble for the both of us. But you left and everything was back to normal. He got on with his life and got over you. But that wasn't good enough for you, was it? You had to come crawling back."

"I don't know what you are talking about."

"Yes, you do! Stop lying! *This* was your plan all along. But I never imagined that you would be so trashy as to bring a baby into this mess. Get knocked up by some random, rich actor for guaranteed payouts and then trap good old Charlie for extra support?"

"You nutcase!" Ruth exploded "How dare you! Yes, it was a mistake—getting pregnant, I mean—but Scarlett was never part of any *plot*. I love my daughter and because of that I have never taken a single red cent from her father."

"Really? Then why were you in LA then? I read that you were spotted around town with *him*." The accusation came out of the blue, completely throwing Ruth for a loop.

"What are you implying, Ita? That I am cheating on Charlie, that I am getting back together with Scarlett's birth father—the man who abandoned his own daughter?"

"I wouldn't put it past a slut," She pointed her finger square in Ruth's chest emphasising the words, "like you."

"You know what, Ita?" Ruth said, grabbing her finger and swatting it away. "What I was doing is none of your business," she continued angrily. "For your information, I *did* see Troy while I was in LA, but it was completely unplanned. I had no idea that he was going to be there. Our time together was limited to reading at the casting agency's office and then dinner that night with the director."

"So you admit it!" Ita declared triumphantly. "You're moving back there. You're leaving Charlie to care for your daughter while you galavant around Hollywood."

"Ita," Ruth said, disgust coming over her face. "You are so ignorant, it's not even funny. I turned down the damn role! I want nothing to do with it. When I saw who my co-star was, I knew I was not going to take the part. Plus, I would never, ever want to leave my daughter and husband behind. They are my family—something I value, but you obviously don't. And this is my home, too. I *live* here Ita—here, in Lakeview. If you have an issue with that, then that's your problem. I love your son, every last bit of him and I always have. I love him because he fills my life with love and happiness, because he is a good father to Scarlett, and because he's going to be a great dad for the children we will have together. I love him because he has always supported and loved me. I cannot trade him in for a career or a chance with someone who let me down more than enough already. Charlie is *the entire reason* for all of it; everything else is just window-dressing. I love your son. The only thing that blows my mind is how such a sweet, caring, wonderful man came from such a hateful, spiteful parent."

With that, Ruth marched off, her words echoing in her own ears. As she made her way back into the dining room, someone touched her arm and led her towards the corner of the room.

"Charlie! You scared me. Where have you been?"

"Listening to you." He pulled her to him tightly, leaning his body into hers. "I am so sorry for how I acted. When you left and I didn't hear from you that night, I let my mother get into my head. I let her convince me that you had this all planned and that you were leaving me."

"Honey, I would never leave you. Ever. You and Scarlett are my life forever and always."

"But what about your career? What if Lakeview isn't good enough for you again?"

She sighed. Now seemed the best time to tell him the news that she had been keeping to herself. "I have some news about that, actually. I wanted to wait to tell you after the party… But I decided that I needed to do something to give back to this community. So, I took some of my savings and took over one of Paul's properties. You know, the old pub just off the square?"

"A … pub?" Charlie looked at her, unsure if he should be mortified or if he should let her continue.

"No. I thought that maybe I could turn it into a stage school. It has all the right bones for it and looks like it would be fairly easy to transform. I wanted to tell you. I really did, but I wasn't sure how to." She waited for a response, but he remained speechless, his face free from any expression or emotion.

"I am going to turn it into a performing school and maybe a theatre, even. It would be free to participate and the shows would raise money for different community causes. To keep costs down, we can even host events there during the off-season like small wedding ceremonies or local event meetings or something. It could really be something special. Are you mad? You should be. I should have told you." She bit her lip.

"You are … amazing," he smiled down at her, completely flabbergasted at this woman and her crazy notions. "Of course, I will support you. This idea sounds amazing. But let's talk about it tomorrow. Tonight is your night."

He took her hand and led her back into the crowd, just in time to watch Ita walk out the door in a huff. Her attempt at slamming the door was completely masked by the roar of the crowd as Ruth took the mic once again.

"This song, I dedicate to my husband, the love of my life forever and always." Ruth turned to Nicky and began to sing one of her favourite Christmas ballads *Have Yourself a Merry Little Christmas.*

And as she sang the lyric about all troubles being out of sight, she looked directly at her beloved Charlie who had picked up Scarlett from the group of happy children and begun to dance.

CHAPTER 29

The carriage bounced up and down and rattled to and fro. But while the snow-covered ride around the lake was rocky, Ella didn't mind. She was too preoccupied with watching the houses and businesses of the community pass her by. The snow was still falling softly in front of them as it covered the shore with a light dusting.

After several minutes of silence, she moved her hand out from under Santa's and turned to face him. She tugged at his beard a bit and pulled off his hat. She knew all along that Joseph would make the perfect Santa Claus.

"Can I ask you a question?"

"Is it how I manage to fit all those presents in my sled?" he chuckled.

"No. I want to ask you why."

"Why what?"

"Why did you give Heidi the balance of the funding? It's just too much. I don't know if I can accept it, Joseph."

"Well, I refuse to take it back, so there is no use in telling me you don't want my contribution." He smiled at her.

"Please, let's just make this a loan. I will pay you back, every penny with interest."

"And I won't accept a cent."

"Be serious, Joseph. I know this is a lot of money we are talking about. There is no way you just had it lying around to give to a friend like me and my lowly little café."

He stared at her long and hard, unsure of how to proceed. Sighing, he said, "You are not my friend."

"What?"

"Ella, I love you. I have loved you for nearly two decades now, but I have never had the courage to say it, never found the right moment to tell you. I'm not trying to use this money, this gift, to buy your affection and you definitely don't have to say it back to me. You're under no obligation. But that was money I had been saving to start a family of my own. It just never happened for me, but now, I know what I want. I want you. I want to be part of *your* family. And I want to help keep this café and everyone who goes there, a family of sorts, alive and going."

She looked at him, studied his face and searched for an answer. Every bit of her was screaming to say something, but she could only smile and hold his hand.

Eventually, she leaned down and nuzzled into the wide expanse of his shoulders. His coat still smelled of pine trees and Christmas.

"If I am going to accept this money, I want you to make me a promise."

"Yeah, and what is that?"

"You will be a partner. And," she held up a hand to silence the protest she knew was coming, "I will not take *no* for an answer. We will be partners in the business—you and me."

"It doesn't seem like I have much of a choice, does it?" he chuckled, kissing the top of her forehead as they snuggled closer together. They passed the rest of the ride in silence, but it was also full of hope and promise that for these two people past the prime of their lives, each day from hereon would be more meaningful with the other in it.

"Here we are, Ella," Eric McGrath said as he pulled the carriage to a halt in front of the cafe side door. Already the next group had lined up, with Heidi giving out instructions and taking tickets.

As they approached, Joseph quickly repositioned his beard and fixed his red hat on top of his head.

Ella led the way as the couple entered the party once more. When Ruth spotted the two, she quickly finished her song and ushered her to the stage.

Standing in front of her beloved community, Ella lowered the mic and spoke again.

"Now for my favourite time of the evening. For all the boys and girls out there, Santa is here! We will be taking pictures and he'll be listening to all of your wish lists. Parents, you can enjoy the famous Heartbreak Café Christmas mulled wine while your children are waiting." She winked. "And it looks like it's going to be a long queue."

The crowd burst into applause and shouts of glee as everyone moved to either the Santa line or the drinks queue while Ruth began to sing some more.

While everyone was preoccupied, Ella snuck out back to her little office. She again searched her desk for the brown envelope of pictures. While most of them she had put on display, she had kept one to herself—the black and white photo of herself and Gregory on the night of their first kiss.

She looked at their faces, so young and full of optimism about the life they had ahead of them. He especially looked as if he could run Lakeview and easily the world. It was that smile. She grinned at the memory of her husband. Running her fingers over the thick paper, she put her lips to the photograph and placed it back in the envelope, knowing in her heart that he would be delighted for her to move on.

It was then that she heard the music start the first few notes of an old familiar song that she remembered fondly dancing to with her Gregory.

She headed outside, past the well-wishers

and in search of Joseph. Unfortunately, she couldn't immediately find him.

All the children had since finished their turns sitting on Santa's lap and were preoccupied with the lollipops he had given them. The parents were still hovering over the mulled wine. The rest of the crowd danced in the centre of the room.

That was when she spotted him—Santa suit and all, out front on the street. She grabbed her coat and joined him outside.

"Joseph Evans," she chided. "What are you doing out here? Come back inside."

He turned to face her, shovel in hand. "If you want me to be a co-owner of this café," he called, "you have to let me keep you safe. The first order of business is keeping the paths clear and free of snow and frost. I wouldn't want anyone to fall—"

Before he could say another word, Ella walked towards him, grabbed the white-trim collar and pulled him in for a long, slow kiss.

The embrace was the first in a very long time for both of them, but she knew that they would learn and love together. It was a kiss filled with promise and meaning, a sign of love that had been growing forever.

And as the snow fell gently around them on Main Street and festive music played in the background, it was, Ella thought to herself, the first of many, many more to come.

FROM THE AUTHOR

Thank you for reading. I very much hope you enjoyed the story.

If you'd like to read more about Ella & the cafe, try a short excerpt of **Days of Summer**, available now.

DAYS OF SUMMER

EXCERPT

CHAPTER 1

Like a wheel of fortune that had last stopped in the depths of winter, the weather had since spun again and laid to rest at where summer sunshine bathed the Irish countryside.

Ella Harris looked up at the clear blue skies and smiled.

It was early June, and today the sun had some real warmth to it for the first time. With days of summer came a lifting of the spirits and a feeling of general optimism.

In her sixty-odd years, she had learned to appreciate all seasons, but summer was without doubt her favourite time of the year.

"Isn't it glorious?" she said to Nina, her friend and part-time waitress in the cafe Ella

CHAPTER 1

ran in Lakeview, a beloved Irish tourist destination.

Twenty minutes drive from Dublin City, the town was centred around a broad oxbow lake from which it took its name. The lake, surrounded by low-hanging beech and willow trees, wound its way around the centre and a small humpback stone bridge joined all sides of the township together.

The cobbled streets and ornate lanterns on Main Street, plus the beautiful one-hundred-year-old artisan cottages decorated with hanging floral baskets, had resulted in heritage designation by the Irish Tourist Board, and the chocolate-box look and feel was intentionally well preserved.

Ella's café was situated in a small two-storey building with an enviable position right at the edge of the lake and on the corner where Main Street began.

Early in their marriage, she and her husband Gregory took over the running of the café from her father-in-law, and Ella had spent nearly every waking moment since then ensuring that his legacy—and that of her dearly

CHAPTER 1

departed husband—lived on through good food, hot coffee and warm conversation.

"Bliss," Nina agreed wistfully. "I adore summer. No more school runs and trying to rush little Patrick out the door in the mornings,' she said fondly, referring to her five-year-old son.

Ella smiled, thinking not for the first time that the younger woman was doing a wonderful job of bringing up her little boy alone. Though she knew Nina had some help from her father - after whom her son was named - being a single mum in a small Irish community wasn't an easy prospect, and she was glad that Nina had overcome her initial indecision about whether Lakeview was the best place to be, as opposed to the city where her mother resided.

Ella was also glad that a few hours a day working at the cafe at busier times helped provide a little extra income for Nina, as well as the opportunity to get out and about. Summer was one of those times.

For Ella, there was no question that Lakeview was the best place to be, but that was easy for her to say. She'd enjoyed a very happy life

CHAPTER 1

here, raised three wonderful children with Gregory and despite burying her husband almost a decade ago had even recently managed to find love again.

She smiled as she thought of the new man in her life - fellow Lakeview native Joseph - and what a whirlwind the last six months had been.

Now, the two women systematically opened each of the ten parasols providing shade for the outdoor seating area overlooking the park by the lake.

Set up for the summer season, the terrace boasted comfortable bistro chairs and tables, plus pretty red and white striped parasols. The cafe's al fresco dining area was now well and truly ready for summer and the town's habitual influx of tourists.

Ella picked up her cleaning bucket and put it next to Nina's before returning inside the cafe through the side door.

As always, the interior felt immediately warm and inviting, with delicious scents emanating from the kitchen.

She stopped to survey the space. The decor hadn't changed much over the years — it was still a warm cosy room with parquet oak flooring, shelves full of dried flowers and old country-style knick-knacks, along with haphazard seating and mismatched tables, one of which was an antique Singer sewing table.

In front of the kitchen and serving area was a long granite countertop, where any solo customers typically nursed coffees and pastries atop a row of stools.

Alongside this was a glass display case filled with a selection of freshly baked goods; muffins, doughnuts, carrot cake, brownies and cream puffs for the sweet-toothed, as well as pies, sausage rolls and Italian breads for the more savoury-orientated.

From early morning the place was flooded with families, friends and neighbours, all there to grab a bite to eat—and to gossip. Ella thrived on the buzz and commotion, and the community embraced her in turn: she had become a bit of a town figurehead and confidant to anyone who came in looking for some conversation with their coffee.

The walls were adorned with watercolours by popular Dublin artist Myra Smith, who routinely spent the days of summer in town

CHAPTER 1

working on her paintings while staying at one of the nearby artisan cottages - many of which were rented out to holidaymakers at this time of year.

The artist had donated a couple of paintings to the cafe as a thank-you a couple of years before, and now even though she was widely famous and sought-after, Myra still popped in now and again.

This room was heavy with memories and all the people whose lives had merged there and Ella reached under her spectacles and dabbed at her eyes.

Why was she so emotional this morning?

Then she remembered that this always happened at the start of summer, before the small community swelled with visitors from near and far, changing the dynamic of both the town and the cafe.

Like every other gone by, Ella hoped that this year's days of summer would be good for Lakeview, and she looked forward to welcoming new visitors whose arrival always managed to create some drama.

"You look so thoughtful," Colm, the cafe's resident chef called out from behind the counter. He was a true gem and had been working for Ella since he was still in school.

She was the first person he'd come out to - a difficult prospect for someone in a small Irish community like this - and they were great friends.

Colm lived with his partner in one of the artisan cottages nearby, but the two men spent a lot of time travelling the world, jetting off at quieter times of the year, during which time Ella held the fort herself.

She chuckled. "Just indulging in past memories. The Heartbreak Cafe has seen its fair share of drama," she joked, referring to the cafe's popular nickname.

Colm rolled his eyes.

"Well, if the last thirty years have been like the last two or three, it must have been crazy altogether," he said, referring to recent personal and community dramas that were somehow always central to this place.

Ella walked a few steps to the front of the counter. The glass surrounding it was sparkling clean; as always Nina had done a wonderful job.

Going out front, she looked up and down

CHAPTER 1

along Main Street. Already there was a hustle and bustle that had been absent over the last few months in the lull between Christmas and early summer.

She saw Paddy Collins walking slowly down the street, his walking stick tapping the ground in front of him.

"Hello Paddy," Ella greeted with a smile. "Time to get out of hibernation?"

He chuckled, the wrinkles around his mouth creasing even deeper. "You're right there. Any chance of a warm cuppa for an ould fella, and maybe an omelette while you're at it?"

"Of course. Come on in."

Ella led the way and duly went behind the counter.

"Cheese and tomato omelette please Colm, our first official customer of the summer is here."

"Our resident swallow?"

Ella nodded. "Yep, it is indeed Paddy."

"OK, then summer has now *officially* begun," the chef declared and retreated to the kitchen.

It was true, Ella thought as a few minutes

CHAPTER 1

later, she arranged the food on a tray, Paddy was as regular as the seasons themselves.

When autumn arrived, he retreated into his cottage and rarely ventured out. He had a daughter, Elizabeth who stayed and kept him company during the harsher winter months. But every year without fail, when the weather changed, almost like a squirrel which had been resting underground, Paddy Collins left his cottage and ventured out, and his first stop was always her cafe.

For the next few months, Ella knew he would eat breakfast at her establishment every single morning and she was only too delighted to have him.

"Is Elizabeth all right?" she asked, placing the tray in front of Paddy. He had chosen the same table he always did, next to the front window where he could watch people passing by on the street outside.

"Oh she's grand, gone up north for a while," he told her.

"Shame that she doesn't spend summer here with us too," Ella commented.

"Ah, I've tried to talk to her but she'll hear nothing of it. Says this place holds too many

CHAPTER 1

memories," Paddy said, cutting up his omelette in a painstakingly slow way.

Ella knew why his daughter avoided being in Lakeview at this time of year. One summer very many years ago, a handsome tourist had come into town and he and Elizabeth had fallen deeply in love. The young couple had spent the summer together, and when it was over, the tourist proposed and they went on to make plans for their future.

The wedding was planned for the following spring, and it was to be the wedding of the year.

Elizabeth's new fiancé returned to Dublin, supposedly to sort out his affairs, but never returned. Paddy's daughter was crushed. She had never truly moved on from that experience, viewing all men as the enemy.

"Maybe one day, she'll find someone else, and get over all that," Ella mused.

"Sure there's nothing I or anybody else can do for her," Paddy muttered, evidently eager to get on with his breakfast.

After that, the café got busy with regulars coming in for breakfast or midmorning coffee.

Around midday, when there was a typical

CHAPTER 1

lull in activity before the lunchtime crowd, a handsome stranger walked in, standing uncertainly in the middle of the room as he scanned the bakery counter.

And here we go, Ella noted smiling, *our first summer visitor.*

DAYS OF SUMMER is available now in print and ebook.

ABOUT THE AUTHOR

International #1 and USA Today bestselling author Melissa Hill lives in County Wicklow, Ireland.

Her page-turning emotional stories of family, friendship and romance have been translated into 25 different languages and are regular chart-toppers internationally.

A Reese Witherspoon x Hello Sunshine adaptation of her worldwide bestseller SOMETHING FROM TIFFANY'S is airing now on Amazon Prime Video worldwide.

THE CHARM BRACELET aired in 2020 as a holiday movie 'A Little Christmas Charm'. A GIFT TO REMEMBER (and a sequel) was also adapted for screen by Crown Media and multiple other titles by Melissa are currently in development for film and TV.

www.melissahill.info

Made in United States
North Haven, CT
21 October 2023